KT-439-769

The Curse of the Chocolate Phoenix

KATE SAUNDERS

MARION LLOYD BOOKS

First published in the UK in 2013 by Marion Lloyd Books
An imprint of Scholastic Children's Books
Euston House, 24 Eversholt Street
London, NW1 1DB, UK
A division of Scholastic Ltd.
Registered office: Westfield Road, Southam, Warwickshire, CV47 0RA
SCHOLASTIC and associated logos are trademarks and/or registered
trademarks of Scholastic Inc.

Copyright © Kate Saunders, 2013
The right of Kate Saunders to be identified as the author of this work
has been asserted by her.

ISBN 978 1407 12987 7

A CIP catalogue record for this book is available
from the British Library

All rights reserved.
This book is sold subject to the condition that it shall not,
by way of trade or otherwise, be lent, hired out or otherwise circulated in any
form of binding or cover other than that in which it is published. No part of this
publication may be reproduced, stored in a retrieval system, or transmitted in any
form or by any means (electronic, mechanical, photocopying, recording
or otherwise) without the prior written permission of
Scholastic Limited.

Printed by CPI Group (UK) Ltd, Croydon, CR0 4YY
Papers used by Scholastic Children's Books are made from
wood grown in sustainable forests.

1 3 5 7 9 10 8 6 4 2

This is a work of fiction. Names, characters, places, incidents
and dialogues are products of the author's imagination or are used
fictitiously. Any resemblance to actual people, living or dead,
events or locales is entirely coincidental.

www.scholastic.co.uk/zone

Praise for Kate Saunders

The Whizz Pop Chocolate Shop

"An enchanting caper"
Amanda Craig, *The Times*

"A rip-roaring adventure story...
Magical and inventive fun"
Observer

Beswitched

"Pure bliss. Don't miss it"
Amanda Craig, *The Times*

"Magic ... time travel ... a funny and
touching story... This book has it all"
Eva Ibbotson

Magicalamity

"An action-packed romp ... Saunders serves up a deeply
plotted, satisfying blend of laughs and thrills"
Financial Times

"Great ... Alan Bennett meets the Brothers Grimm"
The Sunday Times

60000244554

Kate Saunders has written lots of books
for adults and children. She lives in London.

Also by Kate Saunders

The Whizz Pop Chocolate Shop
Magicalamity
Beswitched

The Belfry Witches
The Belfry Witches Fly Again
Cat and the Stinkwater War
The Little Secret

For Martha

Northamptonshire Libraries & Information Service
LONBU

Askews & Holts	

Contents

1

Nicked

It began as a perfectly normal Saturday morning.

Bruce and Emily Spoffard sat in the kitchen reading the papers, while baby Daisy slept in her basket. Their eleven-year-old son Oz (short for Oscar) was upstairs playing with the big Scalectrix track on his bedroom floor, with his best friend, Caydon, who lived across the road. Oz's twin sister, Lily, was in the next bedroom, sorting out her collection of make-up.

Or so they thought.

But nothing at 18 Skittle Street was ever quite normal, and the Spoffard parents had no idea what was *really* going on.

In Oz's bedroom a dirty, whiskery grey rat was riding on top of one of the racing cars. In Lily's bedroom, their daughter was carefully painting the claws of Demerara, a cat they had never seen. And baby Daisy was only sleeping so soundly because the yellow roses on Lily's wallpaper were singing the theme from *Star Wars* – Bruce and Emily Spoffard were deaf to the high, sweet, silvery voices that filled the shabby old house from top to bottom.

When Bruce Spoffard inherited the old chocolate workshop in the busy London district of Holloway, he had known that his ancestors were famous chocolate-makers. But he had totally missed the glaring fact that they were also magic. Though he had been born into a long line of witches, all the family magic had passed him by and jumped straight into his three children. Bruce didn't have a magical bone in his body, and his wife Emily was just the same; incredible events could unfold right under their noses, and they never saw or heard a thing.

"I wish those roses would shut up," Demerara mewed crossly. "They're giving me one of my headaches."

"Daisy loves their singing," Lily said. "Sit still – I don't want blobs of purple nail polish all over my duvet."

"Oh, all right. But you'd better hurry up, dear. Those curlers will be heated by now and I want you to put a couple of small ones in my cheek-fur."

Unlike every other cat in the world, Demerara could talk. She was also immortal, and had lived at the old chocolate workshop since the 1930s. She was a stout, glossy, beautiful animal, with golden-brown fur (her original owner had named her after Demerara sugar) and square, green eyes. Her voice was a weird, shivery, high mewing, with occasional snuffles and yowls. Around her furry neck she wore a gold bell, hanging on a collar of purple velvet.

"And when you've finished my fur, we should do something amusing with *your* hair."

"No, thanks," Lily said. "My hair's amusing enough already."

Lily's hair was dark and wild and curly – her mum said it had a life of its own. She would have loved it to be smoother and more normal, but the cat's ideas for it were usually ridiculous.

"You could plait it into the shape of the Eiffel Tower," Demerara suggested. "That would look stylish. Did I ever tell you about my trip to Paris in 1934?"

The wallpaper choir suddenly started singing the can-can, and Lily giggled so much that she had to stop painting Demerara's claws.

The plump little cat was offended. "Lily, I insist that you do something about your GHASTLY wallpaper!"

"It's not ghastly," Lily said. "Those roses are really sweet these days." When she had first moved into this bedroom a few months ago, the roses had looked like mean faces and whispered spiteful things. They had now become kind and their yellow petals were smiling – but they still enjoyed teasing the bossy talking cat.

"This is the sort of thing that happens when there's too much magic in the house," Demerara snapped. "It soaks into the walls. If I were you, I'd scrape that paper right off and replace it with some nice pink paint."

A loud thump came from Oz's bedroom next door, followed by yells of laughter.

"Good gracious, what are those boys doing in there?" Demerara hissed. "I suppose that vulgar rat is telling rude jokes again – Lily, do my cheeks, then go and tell them to be quiet."

"OK." Lily loved Demerara, but it was sometimes nice to get away from her; this morning she could not stop mewing out orders.

While the nail polish was drying, Lily tackled the fiddly job of putting curlers into Demerara's face fur.

"That should give me some lovely volume," said Demerara, squinting at herself in the mirror. "Now do go and tell them to stop shouting. Will nobody consider my nerves?"

Lily left the immortal talking cat on the bed (looking very funny with her painted claws resting on a pillow and two curlers in each cheek) and went into Oz's room to see what the noise was about.

Oz and Caydon were sprawled across the floor in fits of laughter. A red car was zipping round the Scalextric track, and the dirty grey rat was running along beside it.

"Come on, Spike!" Oz cried. "The car's winning!"

Spike the rat — the other talking animal at Number 18 — flopped down on the carpet, puffing hard. "Cor, I'm all out of breath!"

"Out of condition more like." Caydon gave the rat's stomach a friendly prod with his finger. "You should join a gym."

"Rats don't have gyms," Oz said. "Maybe we should build him one."

"Morning, Lily-girl," said Spike. "I suppose Demerara thinks we're making too much noise. The old boiler's in a right mood today."

Lily knelt down on the floor to pat the rat's greasy little head with her finger. She didn't really like rats, but had got very fond of easy-going Spike. "Don't take any notice — she's only in a mood because she wants to wear lipstick but can't. Cats don't have lips, so it just clogs her fur."

"She's always in a mood," Oz said, grinning. He was Lily's twin. The two of them could read each other's minds, but they didn't look alike. Instead of Lily's wild black hair and dark brown eyes, Oz had straight, light brown hair and his eyes were greenish-blue. "We're only having a bit of fun with Spike."

Spike was also immortal — Oz and Lily's ancestors had

been makers of magic chocolate, and they had used the cat and rat in their experiments.

"No harm in that," Spike said, in his rough, squeaky voice. "With you lot at school all day, it's been too quiet round here."

And at that exact moment, the quiet of Skittle Street was ripped apart by the deafening yatter-yatter-yatter of a helicopter, swooping right down over the roof of Number 18.

The three children rushed to the window in time to see two large black vans pull up outside the house. Suddenly the street was milling with dozens of armed police. Black helmets covered their faces. They wore bulky flak jackets, and their machine guns gleamed in the October sunlight.

"Blimey – talk about speaking too soon!" Spike gasped, jumping on Oz's head to get a better view. "What's going on?"

"Maybe someone in this street is a terrorist," Oz said.

"Or maybe it's a gang of super-criminals," Caydon suggested. "Hey – look!"

Two armed policemen had appeared on the roof of the flats opposite.

There was a tremendous thumping on the front door downstairs that made the whole house shake, and a man's voice shouted, "POLICE! OPEN UP!"

"But we're not terrorists or criminals!" Lily clutched at Oz. "Why're they coming here?"

The three of them hurtled out of the room and down the stairs. Bruce Spoffard was walking calmly across the hall to open the door. He was a tall man, with curly black hair and dark eyes, like Lily.

"POLICE!"

"Dad?" Lily clung to the banister at the bottom of the stairs. "What's going on?"

"Oh, it's probably nothing," Dad said.

A moment later he was lying face down in the hall with his arms spread out, a policeman's foot on his back and a machine gun pointing at his head.

"Dad!" Lily shrieked.

"Hello, officer," Dad said, as politely as he could with carpet in his mouth. "Do come in and have a look round — would you like a cup of tea?" He was acting as if being hurled to the floor by armed police was quite normal.

More armed police — more than Lily could count — charged into the house. Four of them nearly knocked her over as they rushed upstairs, and a moment later she heard the tinny screams of the wallpaper roses in her bedroom. What were they doing up there?

The policeman with his foot on Dad's back held something out to the three children — a small white card, marked with a fingerprint and a bar code.

Oz was the first to get his breath back. "He's from the SMU — that's why Dad is being so calm. This is magic business!"

SMU stood for Secret Ministry of the Unexplained, the unofficial government department that handled anything unexplained that might be a threat to national security. Oz, Lily and Caydon had been recruited by the SMU last summer holidays, when the government had needed their special powers.

"*Wicked!*" Caydon's brown, dimpled, innocent-looking face broke into a beaming smile. "I knew they'd need us again! I knew it! We might get time off school!"

"No!" wailed Lily. "I hate the SMU!" Last summer's work had been extremely scary and dangerous. Oz and baby Daisy had almost died, and she still had nightmares about some of the dreadful things they had seen.

"Sorry, Lily," a woman's voice said. "This is an emergency."

Another armed police officer had come into the hall. She took off her black helmet, and Oz cried, "Hey – it's Rosie! Stop moaning, Lily – it's Rosie from the bomb squad!" The three children knew her from their adventures last summer.

"Shut up," Lily said, "I'm not moaning." But she stopped crying. It was a relief to see Rosie's familiar face, though the pretty young woman looked more serious than usual. She bent down towards Dad, still face down on the carpet. "Sorry about all this, Mr Spoffard."

"Quite all right, officer," Dad mumbled.

"He'll be fine. Please don't worry about him or your

mum," said Rosie. "We've sprayed the street with our special oblivion gas — no non-magic people will notice anything strange, and their memories will be wiped clean and replaced."

"But look, what is all this?" Oz asked. "What's the bomb squad doing here?"

"I'm not in the bomb squad any more," Rosie said. "I've been moved to the SMU special commando unit. We're attached to the SAS and we're here to make a dangerous arrest."

"What — here?"

"There's been a major breach in security."

"But — this has to be a mistake," Oz said. "We don't have any dangerous people in this house!"

Two armed policemen thundered down the stairs. "No sign of her," one of them told Rosie. "She's nowhere in the house and she's not on the roof."

Rosie looked at Lily. "We've come for the cat. You'd better tell us where she is."

2

Cat in Hot Water

"WHAT?" Oz choked. "You've come to arrest *Demerara*?"

"She hasn't done anything bad – she's just a cat!" Horrified, Lily grabbed Rosie's arm. "What're you going to do to her? Why do you need those huge guns?"

Rosie gently shook off her hand. "I'm really sorry. This is how we respond to any Grade One Alert – we've got our orders. Of course we won't hurt her."

"Grade One Alert?" Caydon was bewildered. "But Demerara can't be a threat to national security – all she cares about is food and make-up!"

Rosie said, "Look, I don't like it either. But it really would be easier if you'd just tell us where she is."

Lily's heart skipped, and she felt that Oz was thinking

the same thing – Demerara must be hiding in the magical secret safe in the old workshop; her owner had made it in the 1930s and it was invisible.

They'll never find it, thought Lily.

But her heart sank again a moment later, when Rosie said, "She'll be in the secret safe."

One of the officers held up Spike, who wriggled furiously in his big, black-gloved hand. "Shall we ask the talking rat where it is?"

"You'll be wasting your time!" squeaked Spike. "I'll never tell you. You leave the poor old girl alone!"

"Never mind the rat," Rosie said. "These pre-war cloaking spells are pretty easy to crack nowadays. Get the sensor and the revelation spray."

Lily started crying again. It was dreadful to think of her foolish little cat being flung into some high-security prison with no access to beauty products.

"Stand back, guys," Rosie said kindly. "This could get explosive."

The officer dropped Spike on the floor and went outside to the vans. He returned a few minutes later with a large aerosol can, and something that looked like a very small silver laptop; small enough to sit in the palm of Rosie's hand. She opened it and immediately it let out a deep electronic growling sound.

"In there." She pointed to the door of the old workshop.

The old chocolate workshop, where the Spoffard ancestors had made their magic chocolate, took up most of the ground floor of 18 Skittle Street. Dad planned to make it into an office one day, but for now it was still in a state of perfect preservation, just as it had been in the 1930s. The walls and ceiling were hung with moulds and tools of gleaming copper and silver. There was a deep fireplace, and, in one corner, a large metal cylinder-shaped device, invented by the Spoffards to shake the cacao bean "nibs" from their husks.

When Rosie held the sensor near the cylinder it let out such a deep, violent growl that she nearly dropped it. "Ow! She's here – give me the spray."

Lily, Oz and Caydon crowded into the doorway. Lily clutched Oz's hand; Rosie had found the secret safe that Demerara called her "flat".

The metal cylinder was shoved aside. Rosic shook the can and sprayed it over the blank white wall. She pressed a button on the sensor. "Here we go!"

A loud bang made the house lurch under their feet, and suddenly there was black smoke and an intense smell of burning plastic. When the smoke cleared, the wall had melted away to reveal a stout golden cat, her cheeks in curlers, sitting in a cave filled with rubbish.

"How DARE you!" Demerara screamed. "How DARE you storm into a lady's private boudoir! Close that hole AT ONCE!"

"You're under arrest," Rosie said. "You have the right to remain silent – in fact, we'd prefer it."

"Arrest ME? What on earth for? I haven't done anything! I'm an innocent cat! What's more, I'm a government agent and I DEMAND to see the man known as 'J'!"

"Come with us calmly and quietly," Rosie said, "and if you haven't done anything, you'll be fine."

She took a step towards Demerara. The cat arched her back and bared her teeth. "What am I charged with?"

"I can't tell you. All I know is that you've done something to set off a Grade One Alert, and if you make any more fuss I'll have to use the stun spray."

"Please!" Lily cried out. "Don't spray her with anything!" For a second, she thought she saw a shifty look in Demerara's square green eyes.

"I WILL NOT COME QUIETLY!" Demerara shrieked. Lily had never seen her so angry. "If you lay one hand on me, I'll scratch you to SHREDS!"

"OK, Mike," Rosie said. "She's all yours."

The other officer stepped up to the hole in the wall and made a determined grab for Demerara. The cat let out a strangled yowl of pure fury and stretched her portly golden body like a concertina to slip behind a pile of decayed magazines. The officer flung the pile aside and clamped his hands firmly round her. It was a good thing he was wearing thick gloves – Demerara struggled and scratched and bit, and kept up a stream of angry shouting.

"Take your filthy hands off me! I'll report you — you'll get into trouble for this. You'll be demoted to goblin patrol! I am a SENIOR government agent — I DEMAND that you let me go at once or HEADS WILL ROLL—"

"Take it easy, old girl!" Spike popped his head out of Oz's pocket, where he had been hiding. "We'll get you out of this!"

"Move aside, kids," said Rosie.

Lily, Oz and Caydon were pushed out of the workshop doorway by two more armed officers, carrying a reinforced metal box between them.

Lily was sobbing now. "Can I kiss her goodbye?"

"I'm afraid not. But you'll see her at the interrogation — you three might be needed as witnesses."

"Witnesses to what? She hasn't done anything!"

"It's standard procedure."

"Hang on, I'm supposed to be going shopping with my mum this morning," Caydon said.

"That's been dealt with," said Rosie. "You'll find your new school shoes in your bedroom. Your mum will think you got them yesterday."

"Cool!" Caydon didn't like boring shopping trips for school shoes.

"And I have a violin lesson later," Oz said. He was very good at the violin and enjoyed his lessons — but this emergency was a lot more interesting. He certainly wouldn't be able to think about music while he was worrying about Demerara.

"I'm supposed to be seeing the tutor for my dyslexia," Lily said. "Does she know?"

"Don't worry — you know we deal with everything." Rosie took something from her pocket. Lily couldn't see what it was, until she heard a click and saw Demerara's front paws were firmly clamped into a pair of tiny handcuffs.

"This is an OUTRAGE!" Demerara shrieked. "I will not be paw-cuffed like a COMMON CRIMINAL!"

"Just following orders, Miss." The armed officer dropped the cat into the metal box, and they saw that it was a high-security pet carrier.

"It's a DISGRACE! Children, this is a miscarriage of justice — get me a LAWYER! I demand to see the man known as 'J'!"

"Oh, you'll see J," Rosie said. "He's got a thing or two to say to you. Take her away, lads."

"No!" cried Lily. But there was nothing she could do. Demerara was carried out of the house, and a moment later they heard the vans driving away.

"Phew!" said Rosie, relieved. "Glad that's over. Now for the final clear-up. Lily, you'd better stop crying — your parents think you've signed up for an adventure weekend."

Lily wiped her eyes on her sleeve. She longed to know

what was happening to her cat. But her parents had never seen Demerara, and if they saw her crying she'd have some difficult explaining to do.

It truly was amazing to see how the SMU could control the memories of the non-magic. Dad came into the workshop smiling. "Well, it's a bit of a mess – that gas explosion certainly gave us a shock! But how marvellous of the gas company, sending you lot to clear it up!" he added, turning to Rosie.

The only sign of the dramatic arrest was a small heap of rubbish and broken plaster on the floor.

"My wife's made a pot of tea. . . Lily, what's the matter? It was only a small bang! Poor old Nutella – don't get into one of your states." "Nutella" was his nickname for Lily when he thought she was being particularly nutty.

"I'm fine," Lily said. In the kitchen she could hear baby Daisy crying. Daisy was joined to Oz and Lily by a kind of invisible thread that meant she was feeling what they were feeling.

"We should tell Daisy it's OK," Oz said. "She loves Dem— Er, I mean, she must've been scared by the bang."

They all went into the kitchen, where Emily Spoffard was cuddling the howling baby. The children's mother was a small woman with light brown hair and blue-green eyes, and a slightly faraway look on her face – the after-effect of the oblivion spray, as Oz and Lily recognized from their last SMU adventure.

"I'll take her." Lily held out her arms for her little sister. She loved the baby's warm weight, and the delicious milky, powdery smell of her velvet head.

"Thanks, darling," Mum said. "You're so good at calming her down."

Lily felt the invisible connection and knew that Daisy was worried about Demerara. Though she was a perfectly ordinary baby in every other respect, the smallest Spoffard could read the minds of her big brother and sister. "Shh, shh, it's all right," Lily murmured.

Daisy's downy head was red all over with crying, like a strawberry, but she soon calmed down as she felt the waves of comfort that Lily was sending and went back to her normal pale pink colour.

Mum said, "You're as good as Mary Poppins. Now, let's have that tea."

Rosie put down her machine gun and took off her flak jacket (it was amazing that Mum and Dad noticed nothing at all odd), and sat down at the table for tea and chocolate biscuits.

When she had finished, she smiled at Lily, Oz and Caydon. "We'd better get moving."

"Where are we—?" Lily began. Oz kicked her foot under the table. "Ow!"

"I think it's wonderful," Dad declared. "I had no idea the SAS did adventure weekends for kids!"

The oblivion spray had done its work; Mum and Dad waved them off like a couple of sleepwalkers.

Lily didn't ask again until they were driving off in the black government car. "Rosie, where are you taking us? Will I be able to see Demerara?"

"We're going to a secret interrogation suite," Rosie said. "It's under the unexplained kennels in Muswell Hill."

3

Interrogation

The SMU kennels in Muswell Hill — just a few miles north of Holloway — were a network of high-security underground cages, where all unexplained animals were kept under strict observation.

Lily, Oz and Caydon had been here before, during their last job for the department, and since then Lily had once or twice managed to drop in for a game of ball with Edwin, the ghost of a friendly old elephant from London Zoo. Edwin was mostly invisible, but Lily had actually seen him once, and was always hoping he'd show himself again. In the underground reception area (as dull and bland as the reception area of any office) she ran straight over to the cage that the elephant liked to haunt.

"Edwin?"

Rosie gently touched her shoulder. "Lily, please don't try to summon him. This is a security lockdown, and even an old dead elephant could be a risk."

"Edwin's not a risk!" Lily protested. "He's just a dear old thing who likes to play!"

"Sorry – the three of you have to sit over there while I sign for you and sort out your passes."

Rosie went to the desk and began murmuring to the woman behind it. Lily and the boys sat down on a group of soft chairs in one corner.

Caydon nudged Oz. "This seems like a really big deal. Frankly, I'm a bit scared."

Lily thought of poor Demerara, alone in her reinforced pet carrier. "Me too."

"Yes, but you're always scared," Caydon said. "When I'm scared, it means something."

"Thanks a lot!" Lily mumbled crossly. "You're only braver than me because you're sillier, and you think everything's going to be like a film!"

"Shut up," Oz whispered. He hated it when his sister and his best friend started one of their squabbles. "What I don't get is how one daft little cat could set off a major alert."

"I *know* she's innocent," Lily said. "Though I did wonder if she was hiding something."

"Hmm," Caydon said slowly. "I thought she looked a bit . . . shifty."

"Funny you should say that!" Spike's whiskery head popped out of the pocket of Oz's fleece. "At one point I could've sworn she looked as shifty as one of my rat mates. But search me what she's been up to."

Rosie came over from the desk with three plastic security tags for Lily, Oz and Caydon, plus a tiny one to go round the bedraggled neck of Spike. "Stick close to me, everyone."

The children had never been any further than the reception area. Now Rosie punched a keypad beside a heavy door. It opened slowly and she led them into a dimly lit corridor with shadowy cages on either side.

It was warm here, and there was a smell of sour poo and dirty straw, like a cowshed. They were all very quiet, listening to the howls and growls and screeches that seemed to come from under their feet. These were the sounds of unexplained creatures kept on the floors below.

"I hope everything's safely locked up," Oz said. "What do you keep in here?"

"Don't be nervous," Rosie said. "The cages at this level are low-risk and mostly empty. There's nothing here at the moment except one badger."

"A badger?" Lily relaxed a little. "Badgers are really sweet."

A deep grunt came from the cage right beside her, and an enormous shape suddenly reared out of the shadows and slammed violently against the bars.

21

All three of them yelled and stumbled backwards, treading on each other's feet — this was a badger, but it was the size of a hippo. Frozen with shock, they gaped at the great bulk of matted, muddy grey fur, and the enormous, snapping yellow teeth.

"She was found on Clapham Common," Rosie said. "She attacked a jogger and broke a policeman's arm."

Lily grabbed her sleeve. "Why's she so big? Where did she come from?"

"No more questions — we mustn't keep J waiting."

Lily took a deep breath and made an effort to relax her trembling limbs. (Greta, the tutor she had for her dyslexia, had taught her this method for calming down.) She was very frightened of the gigantic badger, but it was behind bars, and she was getting better at bravery.

At the end of the corridor, Rosie halted at the door of a lift. She hurried them all inside and pressed the single, unmarked steel button. Lily couldn't help letting out a squeak of alarm — the lift hurtled downwards so fast, it felt like falling off a tower.

They came out in another corridor, with another row of cages — occupied this time. The unexplained creatures could be heard stamping and huffing in their straw.

"What's down here?" Oz asked. "More giant badgers?"

Rosie flashed him a grin. "You don't want to know."

"Wow — I do!" Caydon said. "This must be the world's weirdest zoo. Can we see them?"

"Sorry," Rosie said, "You don't have clearance." She punched a keypad in the wall and a steel door swung open, spilling out dazzling white light.

Blinking in the sudden brightness, they walked into a tastefully decorated conference room with a thick carpet and a long, polished table.

"Ah, the three children and the talking rat," said a familiar voice. "Do come in and sit down, then we can start sorting out this hoo-hah."

It was the man known as "J", tall and elegant, with smooth grey hair. Instead of his usual smart suit, he was wearing shorts and trainers.

"Blimey, sir!" Spike said. "I never thought I'd see your knees!"

"The alert caught me in the middle of a game of squash." J was polite and calm, but there was a steely glint in his eye. "Thank you, officer."

"Sir." Rosie saluted and left the room, quickly whispering "Good luck!" in Lily's ear.

Lily asked, "Where's Demerara?"

"And what are we doing here?" added Caydon. "Do you need us for another mission?"

"Not this time," J said. "You're here in case you're needed as witnesses."

"Demerara hasn't done anything bad," Lily said boldly. "There must be a mistake!"

"Sit down here, Lily. Can I get you something to

drink?" It was J's secretary, the woman known as B62. She was about the same age as Lily's mother, and today she was very smartly dressed in a pale blue suit and matching hat. She smiled when she saw Lily staring. "I was at my niece's wedding; it was an emergency scramble." It was nice to see her calm, friendly face again.

"Right — let's get on with it," J said sternly. "B62, I'll have a coffee, two chicken sandwiches and a double chocolate muffin."

"Yes, sir."

It was lunchtime by now and they were all hungry. There were plates of cakes and sandwiches set out on the long table, and they all helped themselves. B62 gave them glasses of orange juice, and Spike nibbled at a lump of cheddar.

"Bring her in," J said.

A door opened and two armed policemen brought in the high-security pet carrier.

"Demerara!" Lily nearly choked on a mouthful of tomato sandwich. "Are you OK?"

"NO, I AM NOT!" Demerara's voice thundered from the depths of her prison cell. "I'm a respected agent of the SMU and I'm being treated like a COMMON CRIMINAL!"

"Demerara," J said. "Kindly shut up."

"How DARE—"

"Speak when you're spoken to. I happen to know that you've been fiddling about with magic chocolate again."

"That's RIDICULOUS!"

Lily and Oz looked at each other uneasily. The cat had a record of "fiddling about" with the Spoffard Brothers' leftover experiments and the results were always disastrous. What had she done now?

"You might as well admit it," J said. "You set off the biggest alert we've had for years."

"Please," Lily blurted out. "Do you really have to keep her locked up?"

"Hmmm, she certainly deserves to be locked up," J said. "Oh, all right," he sighed finally, "let her out." J had a soft spot for the troublesome cat.

To Lily's great relief, the pet carrier was unlocked and out came Demerara, looking very funny with the curlers still in her furious, furry cheeks. One of the officers removed the paw-cuffs. Lily longed to hug her, but J put her down on the table in front of him.

Demerara sighed and stretched. "Well, there's a buffet — I suppose that's something. Lily, dear, just pass me a couple of slices of chicken and—"

"For the last time, be quiet!" snapped J. "You can stuff your furry face AFTER you've done your explaining."

"Pooh," Demerara said sulkily. "I don't know what you're talking about."

"The first charge is failure to report a magical substance. You found some scraps of chocolate left over from one of Isadore Spoffard's experiments."

"All right! I found a few crumbs of old chocolate in the corner of a box. So what?"

"The second and more serious charge," J went on, "is illegal time travel."

"WHAT?" Lily gasped. This was the last thing she had expected to hear. "Demerara's never done any time travel – have you?"

Demerara scowled and looked very sulky indeed. "He can't prove anything."

"Hang on," Oz said. "Our Uncle Isadore dreamed of making time-travel chocolate, but he could never make it work."

"He was too evil," Spike said. "All his experiments were failures."

J sat down. "The crime of messing with the time stream is considered very serious indeed. The normal punishment is a long prison sentence. I won't bother with that if you'll just tell me the truth."

If cats had eyebrows, Demerara would have raised hers grandly. "I haven't a clue what you're talking about."

"The alarm was raised by a professor of history at Oxford University," J said. "He's an agent for the SMU, and during a routine time scan of the library he found signs of what's called 'scar tissue' in the time stream."

"That means he scans all the books for sudden changes in history," B62 said softly, seeing the children's blank faces.

"It means," J said, "that someone has been meddling."

"Pooh and bum," Demerara spat. "How do you know it was me?"

"How do I know?" J was cross, but almost laughing. He pointed at two very old books on the desk, with leather covers wrinkled like tree bark. "The professor found a rare Elizabethan book called *Curiosities of the Court* that was giving a very strange reading on his meter. A whole new chapter had appeared." He looked hard at Demerara. "A new chapter called 'A Catte Speaketh to the Queene'."

"So? It could have been any talking cat!"

"For goodness' sake, Demerara, there aren't any other talking cats! Of course I guessed it was you!" J let out a groan. "You went back in time to the sixteenth century – and met Queen Elizabeth I!"

Lily, Oz and Caydon couldn't help laughing at the thought of that great historical figure meeting their cat, all those centuries ago. "What did she look like?" Lily asked. She was reading a book about the Elizabethans with her tutor, Greta. "Was she wearing her pearls that were the size of eggs?"

"I didn't know she was a queen," Demerara said. "All I know is that I found some chocolate crumbs. I was hungry so I gave them a tiny lick – and suddenly there was a flash of light and I was in the middle of last week. I knew I'd gone back a week because I was just about to eat the lovely tin of Sheba that Caydon gave me. I tried to eat it again, but then there was another flash and it was over. That's how I knew it was time-travel chocolate."

"You should have reported it at once!" J said. "You know the time stream is under constant threat from terrorists!"

"Is it?" Caydon brightened. This sounded a lot more exciting than old books.

"I know why she didn't report it," Spike said. "She wanted to go back in time to see our dear old master, Mr Pierre. Didn't you, old girl?"

The cat bowed her golden head. "I only wanted a little peek at him."

"So you ate the rest of the chocolate?" J asked.

"Yes." Her voice was now a meek little mew. "But it didn't take me back to the 1930s. Instead I suddenly found myself in a very old-fashioned room, full of people in very silly clothes. There was a lady with a painted white face and a dress like a carpet, and she seemed to be in charge, so I asked her for some food. But the more I tried to talk to her, the more everyone pointed and screamed. And then the spell wore off."

"Our history professor thinks the queen was visiting a hunting lodge in Holloway, which was then a tiny village to the north of London," J said. He picked up the larger of the two ancient books. "Demerara's little adventure also explains a new line that has suddenly appeared in one of Shakespeare's plays: 'The catte hath not thy tongue,

Nuncle, but her owne, like the catte at Holwey that ask'd the Queene for sweetmeats.'"

"I was only there for a few minutes," Demerara said, smirking. "I made quite an impression!"

The children were giggling. B62 was trying not to, and even J was smiling.

Lily looked hopefully at J. "It's not too serious, is it?"

"She hasn't done anything that bad," Caydon put in.

"I'm afraid we had to arrest her," J said. "That chocolate could be the most dangerous substance in the world. We need to be totally sure there isn't any more of the stuff."

"Well, there isn't," Demerara said. "I ate it all."

"Thank goodness!" J leaned back in his chair. "Now, Demerara, I want you to think very carefully. What did Isadore Spoffard do with the rest of that chocolate?"

The cat flicked her tail. "I can't think clearly; I'm too hungry."

"Give her some chicken, B62 – it might jog her memory."

B62 took two pieces of chicken out of a sandwich and put them down in front of Demerara, who immediately began eating.

"Pardon me, sir," Spike piped up. "Mr Isadore would have eaten the rest of that chocolate because the experiment was so illegal – he didn't want his brothers finding out what he was up to."

"Mmm, tasty!" Demerara licked her lips. "Is that tuna over there?"

"Good grief. I never thought one small animal could be such a nuisance to my department!" J chuckled unwillingly.

Sensing the emergency was over, Lily asked, "You won't send her to prison, will you?"

"Not this time; it looks like a false alarm caused by a greedy cat and a few leftover crumbs. You can take her home with you."

This was a huge relief. Lily, Oz and Caydon grinned at each other. Lily jumped up and ran over to take the cat into her arms.

"But she'd better behave herself!" J said. He added, in a lower voice, "And let's hope and pray this story doesn't fall into the wrong hands – nobody must know time-travel chocolate existed."

Oz asked, "Why would that be such a bad thing? I'd love to travel back in time. I could stop murders happening, and warn people about earthquakes."

"It's not as simple as that," J said. "Messing about with the time stream is as dangerous as splitting the atom – and luckily, even more difficult. Ordinary terrorists couldn't do anything with that chocolate. But we're not talking about ordinary terrorists." He took a thoughtful sip of tea. "I'll check, of course, just to be safe. Demerara's naughty adventure might turn out to be a blessing in disguise – it's alerted us to something that could be highly dangerous. B62, tell the time-glass boffins to focus on the Spoffard workshop in the 1930s."

"Yes, sir."

"They'll see me," Demerara said. "In my heyday."

J ignored her, trying not to smile. "Tell them I want any information about Isadore's experiments."

Demerara delicately licked her paw. "I expect you'd like to thank me now."

Everyone laughed at this.

"Demerara, you really are incredible," chuckled J. "You've run up a colossal bill – which will probably make the Prime Minister fall down in a dead faint – and you expect me to thank you!"

The cat settled herself more comfortably in Lily's arms. "You said I was a blessing in disguise."

"A very heavy disguise. Now go on, go home, and let's all get on with what we were doing before we were so rudely interrupted." J stood up. "I was winning that game of squash!"

4

A Vision

The emergency was over as suddenly as it had begun. The black government car dropped them all back in Skittle Street, and it was a normal Saturday again. On a normal Saturday afternoon, Oz had his violin lesson with Dr Ludo Spatz, and Lily had a reading lesson with Dr Spatz's daughter, Greta. Violin teachers and private tutors are expensive, but the SMU were paying Oz and Lily's fees as a reward for saving the world last summer holidays (the Spoffard parents thought they'd been given a grant by a charity).

Dr Spatz was not magic. It was the first thing he had told Oz. "I'm a musician, not a wizard. My late wife was a witch, and the SMU gives me a small pension, but that's as far as it goes."

Greta had only mild powers. "I got a little of Mummy's magic," she had explained to Lily. "I have just enough to listen to the news on the magical airwaves, and I can work the enchanted jug she left me – but I'm mainly an ordinary, non-magic teacher. So I'm afraid it'll be long division rather than spells."

Lily didn't care. She had hated her last tutor, and she liked Greta. She was a great teacher. She was kind, and she looked like a real witch, even if her magical powers weren't up to much. Greta had long grey hair and a long sharp nose, and she wore long black dresses and sweeping velvet cloaks; all she needed was a broomstick and a pointed hat.

Greta was a rather nervous person, but today when she opened the door of the garden flat beside the railway line in Gospel Oak, she was more flustered than usual. "Lily – Oz – but you're early!"

"No, we're not," Lily said. "It's exactly three o'clock."

"Is it? Oh, yes, my mistake. Oz, I'm afraid Daddy's just popped out for a moment. Come into the kitchen and I'll make us all a magical drink while we're waiting for him."

The Spatz's flat was dark and crammed with stuff – books, pictures, statues, strange musical instruments. Lily was particularly fascinated by the black-and-white photos of Greta's magical ancestors; her mother seemed to have come from an absolutely huge family and the walls were thick with pictures of very odd-looking people, including a scarily wolfish man with pointed teeth, and a pale semi-nude boy with a tail. The kitchen was like a tidy junk shop, every shelf stacked with china, saucepans and interesting foreign-looking tins of food. Lily sat down in her favourite place at the table, next to an old photograph of one of Greta's ancestors, a woman perched on a broomstick in a huge Victorian dress.

"Dr Spatz didn't tell me he was going out," Oz said. "Do you know when he'll be back?"

"What? Er – not long now!" Greta was flustered again. "What drinks would you like?"

"Chocolate milkshake, please," said Lily. "Just like last time; it was delicious."

"I'm glad you liked it." Greta reached up to a high shelf for her mother's enchanted jug. "To tell the truth, it's my only successful flavour – all the others come out tasting of sprouts."

The jug was large and heavy, made of dull grey metal. Greta placed it carefully on the table. She put the tip of one finger at the bottom of the jug and drew it very slowly upwards, muttering under her breath. Frothy, creamy chocolate milk bubbled up like an underground stream, following her finger until it reached the top and the jug was full. Greta poured the magical milkshake into three tall glasses.

"ARGH!"

Lily nearly spilled her milkshake as a sudden shout broke out. "Who was that?"

"Who was what?" Greta tried to look casual, though it was clear her hands were shaking.

"Someone shouted. A man."

"It came from over there." Oz pointed towards the kitchen door.

"You must've imagined it," Greta said. "I didn't hear a thing."

A loud thump came from inside the broom cupboard next to the kitchen.

Oz stood up. "You must've heard that!"

"Heard what?" Greta's sharp face had turned very pale.

"GRETA!" It was the voice of Dr Spatz, coming from inside the cupboard. "The door's stuck – let me out!"

Greta's mouth fell open. She stood for a moment, gaping foolishly at Oz and Lily.

"GRETA! I know I'm late but I got held up. Open this door!"

Oz said, "Your dad's in the cupboard."

"Oh – er – is he?" stammered Greta, "I mean – yes, he is, I forgot—"

"What's he doing in there?" asked Lily.

"I'll let him out." Oz went over to the broom cupboard and opened the door.

Dr Spatz's thick white hair and blue cardigan were scorched and smoking, as if he had just been pulled off a barbecue. He was very confused when he saw Oz. "Ah – hello, Oz. I was fixing something in here – I must've fallen asleep. Lily, hello—"

His phone fell out of his pocket as he stepped out of the cupboard. Oz bent to pick it up and saw a photo of Dr Spatz on the screen, with his arm around a fat, bearded man in a black suit – a man who looked strangely familiar, though Oz couldn't think where he'd seen him before. He only had time to glimpse the photo before his teacher snatched the phone away.

Dr Spatz smoothed his soot-covered hair. He was a tall, muscular old man, usually far more normal-looking than his daughter. "We'd better get to work, Oz. I want to hear if you've been practising that sonata."

"I want to read more about Queen Elizabeth," Greta said quickly. "And we can both do our calming exercises. Come along, Lily."

The twins were wild to know what was really going on, but Dr Spatz and Greta hurried them into their lessons before they could ask any more questions. After the lessons, Dad came to pick them up, so they didn't have a chance to talk properly until they got home.

"Let's go in your room," Lily said. "I don't want the wallpaper roses to hear us – and I'm quite glad the animals are out. Did Dr Spatz say anything more about why he was in the cupboard?"

"Nothing," Oz said. "What about Greta?"

"Nothing – but I could see that she was nervous. She needed those calming exercises more than I did."

"I didn't believe a word of that lame story," Oz said. "I mean, who goes into a cupboard to fix something and then suddenly falls asleep standing up? And did you get a look at the photo on Dr Spatz's phone?"

"No," said Lily. "What was it?"

"Dr Spatz with a big, bearded guy. I keep thinking I've seen that guy before."

"Where?"

"I don't know; maybe it'll come back to me. Our main problem is what to do next."

Lily asked, "What do you mean?"

"I've been thinking about Demerara," Oz said. He was uncomfortable. "She got into all that trouble because she didn't report something to the SMU. Do you think we should report Dr Spatz and Greta?"

"No!" Lily was indignant. "I'd never report poor old Greta!"

Oz sighed. "I don't like it either – but they're obviously up to something. What if they're breaking the law?"

"We don't know that," Lily said. "It wouldn't be fair to report them just for behaving weirdly."

"You're right," Oz said, relieved. "We don't know their

side of the story. Let's wait till next week and give them a chance to explain."

While the twins were out having their lessons, Caydon spent a couple of hours playing computer games with his friend Ryan, who lived in the maisonette upstairs. He'd planned to spend the rest of the afternoon skateboarding on the slope beside the dustbins. But the October weather had turned cold and blustery, so instead he settled in the small, cosy kitchen to watch Gran cooking.

Caydon's gran, Elvira Johns, worked as a midwife at the nearby Whittington Hospital. She was also a government-registered witch, from a famous family of Jamaican witches. Caydon's mum, Angie, was a totally non-magic bus driver on the number 390, and because she was out at work, Demerara and Spike had joined them for tea. Spike was sitting on a lemon in the fruit bowl and Demerara had curled herself in the most comfortable chair. They were both nibbling cheese and onion crisps.

Gran was a big, comfortable figure with very short grey hair. She was chopping onions so briskly that her large bottom wobbled inside her green tracksuit. It was very relaxing to sit and watch her, after all the drama of the morning.

"I've decided what I want to do when I leave school," Caydon told her. "I want to join the SMU's special commando unit."

"You keep changing your mind," Elvira said, with a deep chuckle. "First you wanted to be in the river police, then the transport police – then it was the magical branch of the bomb squad—"

"This is even cooler."

"Well, I thought they were horrid," Demerara sniffed. "No manners whatsoever – one of them had the cheek to LAUGH whenever I spoke to him!"

"Perhaps he was new," Spike suggested. "It takes them a while to get used to a cat that answers back."

"They had to be strict with you," Elvira said. "You were a naughty girl, darling! The time stream isn't for little cats to mess about with."

"Caydon, dear, I think you should use your magic for something more intellectual and less dangerous," said Demerara. "You could have a lovely posh office in the MI6 building – and you could keep a cosy basket there for me."

Caydon didn't see the point of wasting his magic in some boring office. "Sorry, I don't do the airy-fairy stuff."

He reached across the table for another chocolate biscuit. Just as he did so, a powerful invisible force pulled him roughly out of his chair and hurled him away, beyond the kitchen, into infinite darkness.

"GRAN!" he yelled. "HELP!"

The kitchen was now a tiny patch of light far below him. He stared down at his gran chopping onions, the animals eating their crisps – and himself nibbling a chocolate biscuit.

His first terrified thought was that he was dead.

But if my body down there was dead, it wouldn't be eating a biscuit, he thought; *and Gran wouldn't be chopping onions as if nothing had happened. This must be a dream – even though I feel wide awake.*

Then there was a clapping, fluttering sound in the surrounding blackness and a bird's wing brushed against his face.

"Ow!" he gasped.

Somehow – Caydon couldn't work out where the light came from – he could see the bird moving about in the darkness. What was it doing so busily in the shadows?

He found he could move about, so he edged closer to take a better look. The bird was as large as an eagle, with a curved beak and a crest on its head. It looked as if it were made of dirty metal, like an old brass doorknob. Caydon had a sense that it was ancient.

Then he saw that the bird had a wooden leg, which made it wobble and stagger. It kept vanishing into the darkness and coming back with a beak full of sticks and twigs, which it carefully placed in a heap.

"Oh, I get it," Caydon said. "You're making a bonfire!"

The bird gave no sign that it had heard him. It carried on patiently wobbling to and fro with bundles of firewood, until the bonfire had grown to the size of a small house. It then began to stagger around the bonfire, stopping every few seconds to stare at it closely. Caydon had always thought birds were rather stupid, but this bird looked as clever and serious as a government inspector.

Finally, when it was satisfied, the bird spread its wings and let out a single loud cough. "UGH!"

A small ball of fire, the size of a burning conker, shot out of its beak and into the heart of the heap. The sticks and twigs burst into flames. The fire was so hot and dazzling that Caydon had to take a few steps back.

"Stop!" he shouted. "Get back!"

The one-legged bird limped calmly towards the crackling bonfire and hurled itself into the flames.

"No!" Caydon longed to rescue the foolish bird, but the fire was too hot. He had to watch helplessly while the poor creature burned itself to cinders.

And still the crazy dream went on.

The flames began to form into a fiery shape – huge red-and-orange wings, a long tail that shot out sparks, a burning scarlet beak.

The bird. Caydon somehow knew it was the same bird, though it was now the size of a glider, made of glaring gold, and had two legs. He tried to run away, but the bird bent its big furnace of a head and picked him up in its beak.

"GRAN!" roared Caydon. The inside of the bird's mouth was so boiling hot that one of his trainers caught fire and the phone in his pocket melted like a lump of butter.

Now he was riding on the bird's back, on flat feathers of warm gold. The rushing air suddenly changed, and they were soaring above a bridge in the middle of the city, packed with cars and people.

A woman in the crowd was staring up at them. She looked like an ordinary woman, on her way to work with a briefcase and a cup of coffee, but the expression on her face was dreadful. Caydon understood, for a few horrific seconds, what real wickedness looked like.

But now they were shrinking and the people on the bridge were growing. The wicked woman opened her briefcase; it yawned at them like a leathery cave, a huge Marks & Spencer chicken and pesto sandwich in one corner.

"Stop!" Caydon squeaked, as the bird flew into the depths of the woman's briefcase.

The bird, the briefcase and the bridge vanished, and he was spinning madly through endless darkness.

"Caydon? Good grief, child, what's got into you?"

The darkness had changed into the big brown face of Gran, a couple of inches from his own. He was back in the kitchen, wide awake and very out of breath. Demerara and Spike were gaping at him with their mouths open.

"Cor, you gave us a turn!" Spike gasped. "I nearly choked on my crisp!"

"My dear Caydon," Demerara said, "I only made a suggestion – you didn't have to let out a blood-curdling scream!"

"Did I scream?" Caydon checked his burnt trainer and melted phone, which were now totally normal.

Gran pinched his cheek. "Young man, I think you've had your first vision! Well, well, seems like you might have some airy-fairy talents after all!"

"What are you talking about?"

"We haven't had visions in the family since my great aunt Iris!" Gran beamed proudly. "Tell me what you saw. Don't leave anything out."

She turned down the gas under her sauccpan and sat down at the table. Caydon told everything he had seen.

"That bird was a phoenix," Demerara said. "You'll know about them from those Henry Porter books."

Caydon snorted with laughter. "Harry Potter!"

"Whatever," sniffed Demerara. "A phoenix is a magical bird that lives for a thousand years and then burns itself on a bonfire. And then it rises from the ashes as good as new. That's what you saw."

Gran frowned, deep in thought. "I wonder what it means? Visions always mean something. It could be something important, or just something small – Auntie's visions used to remind her to pick up her dry-cleaning."

"Hang on!" Spike dropped the crisp he had been holding in his front paws. "I've just had a thought!" His whiskers were quivering with excitement. "After one of his failed experiments Mr Isadore had a lot of leftover chocolate. It made him feel so sick he couldn't eat it—"

"Good heavens, yes," Demerara said. "Well done, Spike! I didn't think you rats had such good memories, what with your brains being so tiny."

Spike chuckled squeakily, not at all offended. "Yep, it's pretty small as brains go. What happened to that chocolate, old girl?"

"I think he made it into a statue," Demerara said, her square eyes narrowing in concentration. "He was famous for his chocolate sculptures."

"He certainly was." Elvira, who had once been married to the evil Isadore Spoffard, sighed. "When we got engaged he made me a beautiful chocolate Venus de Milo. But that wasn't magic; it melted in the Jamaican sun before I could eat it."

"I've got it!" Demerara slammed down her paw on the table, shattering her crisp. "It's all come back to me! He made the failed experiment into a big chocolate bird! Dear old Mr Pierre thought it was vulgar because Isadore covered it with edible gold leaf."

"A golden bird," Gran said. "A gilded chocolate phoenix – that's what you saw! Now, Demerara, think hard – what happened to it?"

"Isadore took it to Paris, where it won a Silver Medal at an exhibition. Afterwards he got drunk on champagne and his girlfriend stole it."

"Hmmm." Elvira frowned. "So there's a golden phoenix, made of illegal time-travel chocolate. Your vision might mean that it's still at large. I'd better make a full report."

5

Identity Parade

"I'm glad things are back to normal," Caydon said, as they were making their way to assembly on Monday morning. "Demerara's arrest was a laugh — but that vision freaked me out. And Gran keeps saying it's a 'gift'. She wants me to get a posh office job at the SMU when I leave school — and I want a job with a bit of action, where I get to have a gun."

"I'd have been terrified," Lily said, with a shiver. "I wonder what your vision meant?"

"Gran said it was probably nothing. But she made a full report anyway, and sent it to be analysed."

"How do you analyse a vision?" Oz asked.

"I don't know and I don't care. I don't want a special gift and I'm still joining the commando unit."

"Caydon Campbell," Ms Shah called. "What part of 'No Talking' do you not understand?"

Their class, 7Shah, was filing into the assembly hall at Sir Richard Whittington School, and pupils were supposed to be silent.

At first, when she had started at the school half a term ago, Lily had been a bit scared of the hall where they had assembly. It was much bigger than the hall at her primary school; Sir Richard Whittington had more than a thousand students. But she was getting used to it, and she liked her new school. The girls here were nicer than the girls at her old school, for one thing — Lily had already made a few friends, and her dream was to find one magic enough to see Demerara and Spike. *It would be great to have another girl to talk to*, she thought. *Demerara's lovely, but there are things she just doesn't understand, and it's not normal to have a best friend who's a cat.*

The Year Seven classes sat in the front rows of the hall, near the stage. On the stage sat Ms Bolt, the headmistress, Mr Olewame, who taught PE and was a judo champion, and Mr Trimble, who taught science.

Lily was already drifting away into a daydream when she heard Ms Bolt shouting out her name.

"Oz and Lily Spoffard and Caydon Campbell," the headmistress called. "Stand up."

The three children glanced at one another uneasily.

Were they in some kind of trouble? There was something very wrong with the way Ms Bolt looked, as if she'd lost control of her own face. It was normally a kind face, and now it was stern and mean.

"Come to the front," said Ms Bolt. "Nice and slow — and keep your hands where I can see them."

Oz whispered, "What's going on?"

"MOVE!" yelled Ms Bolt. Her normally good-humoured voice had the sting of a whiplash.

Everyone else packed into the hall — teachers and kids — were as still as statues and deathly quiet.

Lily nudged Ruby, the girl sitting next to her. Ruby didn't move. She was staring vacantly into space.

"This is magic," Oz said.

"But it can't be," Lily said. "We're at school!"

"RUN!" shouted Caydon.

He pushed along the row of seats and made a dash for the doors at the back of the hall.

"Get him," said Ms Bolt.

Caydon was a fast runner, but he couldn't compete with Mr Olewame and Mr Trimble. The two muscular teachers pelted after him so fast that they were almost blurred like people in a speeded-up film. With growls of fury they grabbed Caydon's arms and carried him — struggling with all his might — back to the platform.

Oz made a brave leap at Mr Olewame; the judo champion brushed him off like a fly.

"Look!" Lily cried out. "Something's happening to Ms Bolt!"

The round, friendly face of the headmistress was changing into another face – a dreadful face, with black eyes like dots of concentrated poison.

"It's HER!" Caydon gasped.

Suddenly, the huge window at the end of the hall exploded in a shower of broken glass; the shards instantly changed into falling snow before they could hurt anyone. Dozens of armed police poured through the window.

"CURSE YOU!" roared Ms Bolt. "MY CURSE UPON YOU ALL!"

There was a sickeningly bright flash of light; for one fraction of a second, Mr Olewame and Mr Trimble changed into snarling, snapping wolves – and then the three false teachers vanished.

Lily rushed to hug Oz and Caydon. "Are you OK? Did they hurt you?"

The armed police began to walk through the silent rows of schoolkids, spraying them with huge aerosol cans. Two officers jumped on to the stage and pulled aside the curtain to reveal the real Ms Bolt, Mr Olewame and Mr Trimble, bound and gagged and stripped to their underwear.

"OK, everyone – well done!" One of the armed raiders took off her helmet. It was Rosie. She gave the twins and

Caydon a reassuring grin. "I didn't think I'd be meeting you lot again so soon!"

"What was that?" Oz asked faintly.

"No time to explain now, I'm afraid. You're going straight into protective custody – there's a helicopter waiting for you in the playground."

"It was HER!" Caydon was trembling. "I'd know that face anywhere – it's the woman I saw in my vision!"

"I've never seen you as scared as this," Lily said. "Normally I'm the one who shakes and gets hysterical."

"Bog off!" Caydon snapped. "I'm not hysterical."

"You should take a deep, slow breath, counting up to ten—"

"I know how to breathe, thanks."

"It's the calming exercise Greta taught me."

"Well, I don't need it, OK? I'm totally calm – calmer than you are."

"Shut up," Oz said. "Both of you. Don't start one of your stupid arguments now." He was very pale. "You saw what happened, didn't you? We came this close to being kidnapped."

The SMU helicopter was an army model without windows. Lily, Oz and Caydon were strapped tightly into hard seats, with nothing to look at except one another's freaked-out faces.

"I just don't get it," Caydon said. "Why would anyone

want to kidnap us? Why is that woman in my vision picking on ME?"

The helicopter began to drop to the ground. They had been taken from the school playground to the SMU safe house, a sprawling mansion beside the sea, where all kinds of magical experts worked round the clock against the forces of the unexplained. They knew the safe house, and it was a relief to be back inside the high-security grounds.

"I'm hungry," Oz said. "I hope they let us go to the canteen."

"I hope Mum and Dad are OK," Lily said. "And Daisy."

"We'd know if something had happened to Daisy," Oz said. "We'd feel it."

The door of the helicopter opened and cold, sea-smelling air gusted into the cabin. Rosie guided them out. They had landed on a helipad at the top of a cliff, and they shivered as the salty wind whipped at their clothes. The waves crashed on the rocks below, and seagulls wheeled and screamed above them.

Rosie led them to the grand entrance hall of the building, which had a marble floor and walls covered with old paintings, like a stately home.

B62 was waiting for them. "Oh, I'm so glad you're all right!" She beamed at them all, and at Rosie. "J says very well done, officer — that was a superb operation."

"Thank you, ma'am." Rose unstrapped her machine

gun. "Phew, I'm parched! I'm going straight up to the canteen for a cup of tea – anyone want anything?"

"Don't worry about that," B62 said. "We've got refreshments laid on – come into the library."

The library was a large room, lined with old books and with a splendid view of the grey sea and sky.

"Gran!" Caydon pelted across the room to hug Elvira, who was standing beside the window in her midwife's uniform. She had obviously been summoned in a hurry – she was still wearing a plastic apron. She hugged Caydon so hard that his trainers lifted off the floor. She hugged Lily and Oz too.

"Well, you're safe and sound," a familiar voice mewed. "And now that you're here, perhaps we'll FINALLY get something to eat." The plump, sleek, golden-brown cat jumped gracefully off the mantelpiece.

Lily bent down to stroke her. "What are you doing here?"

"I'm not in trouble this time," Demerara said smugly. "I'm helping."

The man known as J stood up from behind his desk. "I'm so glad to see you all. We got you out just in time! B62, bring in the tea and biscuits, please. These children have had a shock."

"Yes, sir." B62 left the room.

Demerara said, "I've had a shock too. I'd like to remind you that even immortal cats have to eat. And I haven't had a SINGLE BITE since Lily gave me her egg this morning."

"Demerara," said J, "it would be nice if you could stop going on about food for just five minutes."

Oz asked, "Where's Spike?"

"Spike stayed behind in Skittle Street. He's raised an army of one hundred thousand sewer rats, and they're packing out every drain in Holloway. No terrorist will slip past them."

"Terrorist?" Oz was alarmed. "What about Mum and Dad, and Daisy? Are they OK?"

"And my mum? It's her day off today," Caydon said. "Look, what's going on?"

"Please don't worry," J's tone was serious. "Everyone's safe — for the moment, at least. It's one of the biggest operations we've ever mounted."

B62 came back into the room, pushing a trolley laden with teacups and plates of biscuits. Lily didn't really like tea, but she was thirsty enough to drink the cup that B62 put into her hand. This tea was sweet, with a nice aftertaste of toffee, and it made her feel less swirly-headed.

Demerara was given a saucer of posh salmon cat food, and immediately stopped being in a huff.

J took a bite of Rich Tea biscuit. "As you've all gathered, this is a national emergency."

Oz asked, "How did the SMU know we were about to be kidnapped?"

"It was Caydon's vision. Our experts analysed it and spotted something that meant you three were in mortal danger."

"How do you analyse a vision?" Caydon asked. "Did the experts see it too?"

"It's complicated," J said. "They can't actually see it, of course. Basically, they examine the symbols in the vision. Yours seems to mean that Isadore's golden phoenix has fallen into the wrong hands. And those wrong hands want you three because you have the power to channel the magic of the Spoffard triplets, without which the phoenix is quite useless. Thank goodness Elvira reported it in time!" He shot a stern look at Demerara. "Now you see how vital it is to report anything suspicious."

"There's no need to go on about it," Demerara said crossly. "For the last time, I didn't report the chocolate because it didn't seem important."

"It's not your job to decide what's important," said J. "Your job is to report any unauthorized magic, no matter how small." He turned his stern gaze upon the three children. "Have any of you seen anything odd recently – anything at all?"

Lily felt her cheeks turning hot and she avoided looking at Oz. They were both thinking about Dr Spatz and Greta. But they couldn't be tied up with all this. She shook her head.

"It would be very helpful," J said, "if we could identify

the woman in Caydon's vision. We don't know what she looks like, but you three all saw her this morning. I'm going to show you some mugshots from our criminal files." He pressed a button underneath his desk. The tall bookcase behind him slid open to reveal a large screen. "Tell me if you recognize any of these faces."

What they expected to see were identikit photos of people's faces, like you saw in crime dramas on television. But the first picture that flashed up on the screen was an old vase, with a label that said "AD 400".

"Take your time," J said.

Caydon stared at the screen. "But that's just a bit of pottery!"

"Look at the faces."

There were painted figures on the vase, of women in long white dresses. The faces of these women were crudely drawn, but when you looked closely each one was slightly different.

"Maybe the one in the middle," Caydon said.

The painted face in the middle of the group was the largest, and her slanted eyes were as wicked as a drawing could be – though Oz and Lily couldn't see that she looked like anyone in particular.

"Thank you," said J.

A new picture appeared on the screen. This time it was of a mouldy old piece of stone, faintly carved with figures of dancing women.

"Byzantine, from the fourth or fifth century," J said. "This item is in the British Museum."

"Why are you showing us antiques?" Oz wanted to know.

"Hush, darling—" Elvira took a step closer to the screen. "That one on the end—"

"On the left," Caydon said.

The figure on the left was almost rubbed smooth and hardly had any face left at all, but he sounded very sure.

The next picture on the screen was a medieval painting of a king being crowned by a bishop, watched by a group of people in one corner, squashed into a sort of wooden pen.

"From fifteenth century Hungary," J said. "I'll zoom in on the crowd."

The cluster of medieval faces now filled the screen.

Caydon and Elvira gasped, and Oz and Lily cried out together – "There – in the middle!"

This face had been painted hundreds of years ago, with only a few lines of paint, but there was no mistaking it – it was the same evil face they had seen in assembly.

"I was afraid of this." J's face was grim. He suddenly looked years older. "I've hoped and prayed this was an enemy I'd never have to face again. I'm going to flash through a few more pictures. If you see her, just say 'Yes'."

The screen showed a series of pictures that went

through the ages, from Roman carvings to modern photographs – and the evil face was in all of them. They saw her in a painting of a crowd at a public execution, and she was grinning in a group photo of guards at a concentration camp. She popped up in all the big events in history through the ages, from the Roman Empire to the Second World War.

"It's one of them," Elvira said, breathing hard. "Secunda?"

"I think it's worse," J said. "I think it's Alba herself."

"No!"

"Gran?" Caydon grabbed her hand. "Who're you talking about? Who's Alba?"

J took a deep breath, as if he were doing Greta's calming exercise. "I won't go into details now, but that woman belongs to the deadliest criminal organization on the planet. B62, tell the SMU sections of the emergency services to cancel all leave and stand by."

"Yes, sir," whispered B62.

"Tell the ghost manager to send a squad of armed psychics to protect the Royal Family and all Members of Parliament."

"Yes, sir."

"Warn all departments. This is a Code Red – D33 is back!"

6

Burning Alba

"D33 doesn't *sound* like a criminal organization," Caydon said. "It sounds more like a bra size."

"Don't be cheeky — this is a very serious business." Elvira was stern, trying to hide how worried she was. "When you find out about D33, you won't want to joke about it."

"I don't understand why we need blood tests," Lily said. "I hate needles."

"You're being tested for certain magical antibodies. Don't worry, it won't hurt."

Elvira was taking Caydon and the twins to the medical room. They were walking along a blank office corridor, which looked perfectly ordinary until you saw the signs on the doors: GOBLIN CONTROL, SHAPE-SHIFTING, VISION

ANALYSIS (LEADING TO DREAMS), TIME-STREAM ANALYSIS. One door, labelled WEATHER, was slightly open, and they saw a room filled with a lashing tropical storm. Lightning zig-zagged across the ceiling, rain battered against the filing cabinets, and there was a man at a desk, eating a sandwich under an umbrella. Another door said GHOSTS, and they were all startled when a woman walked right through it, holding a ghostly cup of tea.

"This is my old office." Elvira halted suddenly in front of a door that said TIME GLASS READERS. Her frown melted and she smiled. "I worked here for six whole months."

"But—" Caydon was bewildered. "You work in a hospital!"

"It was before you were born, darling – before your mum was born. I'd just come over from Jamaica, and I couldn't start training to be a midwife until I'd done some National Service in magic. I had a special gift, you see. I can read a time glass."

"Gran? What are you talking about?" Caydon was staring at his grandmother as if he'd never seen her before. "What's a – a time glass?"

Oz said, "It's a way of looking back at the past. I saw Uncle Isadore do it once. You set a date, and a picture of the past appears, like a film."

Elvira looked at Oz thoughtfully. "You could see the picture, could you? Not everyone can. Well, well, you twins certainly inherited a lot of magic." She halted in front of a door that said MEDICAL ROOM and ushered them all inside.

It was a bare white room that looked and smelled just like the medical room at school. Lily was the most worried about the blood test, so Elvira did her first. She picked up one of Lily's fingers, gave it a tiny prick with a needle and squeezed out a bead of blood, which she carefully smeared on a piece of paper.

"See? Didn't hurt a bit. Give me your fingers, boys."

Elvira took drops of blood from Oz and Caydon and turned away from them to label their pieces of paper.

And then, out of nowhere, Caydon let out an agonized scream.

"Caydon?" Oz grabbed his friend's arm.

Caydon was on fire. Orange flames leapt out of his legs, his shoulders, his head. Oz looked down and saw flames dancing on his own sleeves. He saw Lily burst into flames – her mad hair was a great burning bush. More flames shot out of the corners of the medical room, and the sea outside the window was a boiling mass of fire.

The fire didn't hurt, but it gave Oz a horrible feeling inside, as if hard fingers were rootling in his most secret thoughts. He was scared to the core of his bones, and could feel Lily's terror, and Caydon's. He felt as though the three of them were stuck together in an invisible red-hot circle.

Through the bars of flame, he saw Elvira shouting and waving her arms.

A moment later, a blissful lightness and coolness spread through the circle – and everything was normal again. Oz, Lily and Caydon were shocked and breathless, staring round at the calm white room and the flat grey sea outside.

"What – what was that?" Lily was pale and her voice was a squeak.

"Caydon had another vision," Elvira said. "And you two picked it up like a radio signal."

"Did you pick it up too?"

"No, darling. I guessed from the looks on your faces, and said a quick neutralizing spell. Caydon – can you hear me?"

"Course I can," Caydon said faintly. "You don't have to shout." He tried to sound cocky, but he was trembling.

Elvira shook some white powder into a glass and added water. The mixture in the glass fizzed violently and turned deep purple. She gave the glass to Caydon. "Drink this."

"Yuck!" He made a face. "It smells like old trainers!"

"Don't argue, young man."

Caydon drank the purple mixture and immediately stopped trembling. "I'm really hungry now. Can we go to the canteen?"

"We'll have to take this straight down to Vision

Analysis," Elvira said, shaking her head. "I don't like it at all."

It was ages until the children were allowed to go to the canteen. Elvira took the blood samples to the lab for testing. She then marched them down the corridor to Vision Analysis. Here they were shut into dark booths like old phone boxes, with electrodes stuck to their heads, and told to remember exactly what they had seen – which was difficult when they were tired and hungry.

The sea and sky were darkening by the time they queued with their trays at the twenty-four-hour canteen and sat down at a table beside the big window.

"I saw the bird again," Caydon said. "It crashed out of a cupboard in the medical room and grabbed me in its fiery beak – me and you two. We were flying over the same bridge I saw last time. The whole city was burning. The people were screaming. It was horrible."

"I didn't see any of that," Oz said.

"Nor did I," said Lily. "I just saw you and Oz in flames. I wish I knew what was happening. I want to go home."

They were not allowed to stay long in the canteen. Before Caydon had finished his chocolate mousse, Elvira hurried them off to an underground bunker, built deep into the cliff.

Demerara was sitting on the desk, very cross. "They

wouldn't let me come to the canteen. I had to sit with a lot of wires on my head while they did memory readings."

"For goodness' sake, Demerara," B62 said. "I brought you lunch!"

"Oh, was that tiny saucer supposed to be lunch? Pardon me, I thought it was just a SNACK."

"Demerara," J said, "for the last time, kindly keep that furry mouth shut. This is very serious. I've just had the results of the blood tests – and all three of you are carriers of the D33 gene. This might explain why they tried to kidnap you."

Oz, Lily and Caydon looked at each other blankly.

Caydon asked, "Does that mean we're evil?"

"It's more complicated than that." There was a large screen on the wall. J pressed a button and a picture appeared – a stone head of a man with a beard. "This is the third century Roman Emperor Diocletian."

"Pooh," said Demerara. "Another history lesson."

J gave her a stern look. "The Emperor Diocletian married a witch and together they had thirty-three very wicked daughters. Diocletian found them thirty-three husbands, but the wicked girls murdered them. The Emperor was at his wit's end, so he banished them to a rainy, windy island in the north, where they intermarried with the local giants. The island was named Albion, after the oldest daughter Alba, the wickedest of the lot."

"The woman from my vision," said Caydon. "The woman on the bridge – the woman who disguised herself as Ms Bolt—"

"Yes, that was Alba. 'Burning Alba' they call her, because she loves starting fires. We've been trying to keep her out of this country for as long as I've been working at the SMU. But this is her home. 'Albion' is an old name for Britain."

Lily shivered. She had a sudden sense of something awful looming ahead, like a gathering storm. "Does the blood test mean we're related to her?"

Oz nudged Caydon. "Hey – maybe it means we're related to you!"

"Two of the wicked daughters, Nona and Undecima (nine and eleven in Latin), met a saint during the sixteenth century and suddenly turned good," J said. "Undecima stayed in Albion and one of her descendants married a Frenchman named Spoffard. That's why you twins carry the gene."

"And Nona went to Jamaica," Elvira said. "Where she built herself an invisible castle on top of the Blue Mountain. She is my ancestor – so you three are very, very distant cousins."

Oz stared at Caydon's brown face, Caydon stared into Oz's white face, and they burst out laughing.

"Cool!" Caydon said. "I always thought we looked a bit alike!"

"That means you're our distant cousin too," Lily said, smiling shyly at Elvira.

"Yes, darling," Elvira said. "We're all descended from the same wicked witch – and a Roman emperor. But I don't carry the same special gene."

"We think Alba's using the D33 genes in you three children as tracking devices," J said. "Which is why we've decided to send you back to Skittle Street. We can't risk Alba and her evil gang finding out about this place."

"You mean – we can go home?" Lily was longing for home, and Mum and Dad, and Daisy. "Will it be safe?"

"You'll have full protection," said J. "Spike and his rats are down in the drains, and I've already sent in a squad of armed ghosts to patrol the street without disturbing any non-magic people."

"How can ghosts be armed?" asked Caydon. "Are their guns ghostly too? And the bullets?"

"The bullets won't hurt ordinary people. They're special supernatural bullets."

"But we won't be able to go to school," Oz said. "It'll be too dangerous."

"I'm posting one of my strongest bodyguards at your school," said J. "Look out for someone new tomorrow morning. I'm leaving you in the hands of an expert."

7

Silver

"I don't understand," Oz said. "There aren't any new teachers. What happened to that bodyguard we were promised?"

"He'd better be big and strong," Caydon said. "D33 are bound to try again." He wasn't his usual bouncy self this morning. "I didn't dare go to sleep last night, in case I had another of those visions. And now I'm terrified they'll try to kidnap us again."

Caydon, Oz and Lily were walking into their classroom after assembly. It was weird being back at school. Nobody remembered a thing about yesterday's commotion. Ms Shah thought they'd all been away with colds.

"Settle down, everyone!" called their teacher. "We've got someone new joining us today." She smiled at a skinny girl, with long, rather dirty blonde hair, standing beside her. "This is Silver Biggins. Silver, go and sit down over there – next to Lily. I hope you'll all make her feel welcome."

Lily stared at the new girl. Silver Biggins wore a baggy denim skirt, a rainbow jersey full of holes, and generally looked like a grimy hippy at a rock festival. Oz and Caydon, on the other side of the classroom, made faces at Lily to show they were thinking the same thing. There was no way this girl could be their bodyguard.

Silver was carrying a backpack, covered in an amazing array of biro-scribbles and key rings. She thumped it down on the floor and took the empty seat beside Lily. Up close, Lily could see she wore a dirty brass bell around her neck, tied on a frayed piece of purple ribbon.

"Hi," Lily said politely.

"Hi," said Silver.

"SETTLE DOWN!" Ms Shah called again. "Look at the whiteboard, please, and not at the new girl. Let's see if any of you can remember how to multiply fractions."

Lily had worked on this as hard as anyone else, but it had all flown out of her head – she had the sort of dyslexia that makes you struggle at maths. Ms Shah might as well have been talking gibberish, and Lily started doodling on her notebook.

Silver's hands were clasped on the table in front of her. Very slowly, she pulled something out of one bedraggled rainbow sleeve and put it down in front of Lily. It was a plastic card with a bar code and fingerprint: Silver Biggins was working for the SMU.

Lily was so surprised that she gasped aloud. "What?"

"Shhh!" Silver whisked the card out of sight like a conjuror. "Later."

Surely this couldn't be their bodyguard! The SMU wouldn't send an eleven-year-old girl to protect them from the dark forces of D33.

Lily waited impatiently until the bell rang for morning break. There was a surge for the door, and the racket of talking and scraping chairs made it safe to talk. She turned to Silver. "You're in the SMU?"

"Yes," Silver said. "I've been assigned to bodyguard duty. I've got to stick close to you – it'll help if we act like best friends."

"Oh." Lily was confused. "Is it just you?"

"Yes."

"J said he was sending an expert."

"That's me," Silver said calmly. "I do all the really tough cases."

"Oh."

"I protect the queen on Walpurgis Night. That's how good I am."

The classroom was empty now, except for Oz and Caydon, who were waiting for Lily beside the door. Silver briefly flashed her SMU card at them.

"What?" gasped Caydon. "You? They have got to be joking!"

Silver stood up, shouldering her mad backpack. "Keep your voice down or you'll blow my cover."

"But, you see —" Oz didn't like to hurt anyone's feelings, but felt he had to say it "— we were expecting someone — well — a bit older."

"A lot older," Caydon said, eyeing Silver suspiciously.

"I'm two hundred and forty-six," said Silver.

"Yeah, right."

"But I'm stuck at eleven for all eternity because I'm a vampire."

"Get off! Do we look that stupid?"

Silver grinned at them. For a moment, it made her face surprisingly pretty. But then her grin widened, her lips reddened and her smile stretched into an animal snarl, her teeth changing into long, lethal-looking fangs. Lily squeaked and hid behind the boys.

"Relax." Silver's fangs had disappeared and she was chuckling. "I'm not going to bite you — we don't do that stuff any more."

"Are those *Twilight* books true then?" asked Caydon "Are you a vegetarian vampire who only drinks animal blood?"

"I don't drink any sort of blood," Silver said. "Vampire symptoms can be treated nowadays. We take medicine and go to a special clinic. It's a bit like diabetes."

Now that he had got over the first shock of meeting a genuine vampire, Oz was interested. "Does that mean you've been cured?"

"No," Silver said. "There's no cure for being one of the Nosferatu. But it means we can live among normal people without sucking their blood."

"I hope you're telling the truth about that," Caydon said. "Otherwise we'll have to kill you by driving a wooden stake through your heart."

Silver grinned. "You could try!" There was no one else in the classroom, and so she grabbed the front of Caydon's sweatshirt, whisked him into the air and held him above her head like a sack of feathers. Oz and Lily burst out laughing at the amazed look on his face when Silver set him back on his feet.

"Wow!" Caydon was breathless.

"Don't worry, I won't do it again," she told him. "I just had to show you that I'm not your average eleven-year-old girl. I have superhuman strength. You can trust me to take care of you."

"I thought vampires couldn't go out in daylight," Oz said.

"That was dealt with years ago," said Silver. "We have a special injection every full moon."

"If you're stuck at the age of eleven for all eternity, does that mean you have to go to school for all eternity?" asked Lily.

"I'll answer questions later," Silver said crisply. "Just carry on doing whatever you always do, and ignore me."

It was impossible to ignore Silver. She took her duties as a bodyguard very seriously. Wherever they went, she darted ahead of them to check the place for magic. She had a grubby plastic thing like a thermometer, which she swept across walls, trees and benches. To the great annoyance of Oz and Caydon, she even insisted on checking the boys' toilets. At lunch she sat with them and held her plastic thermometer over their food. At the end of the day, she walked out of school clinging to Lily's arm.

"It's a good thing you don't have any proper friends. You'd be much harder to guard in a crowd."

"Ow – let go!" Lily tried to pull her arm away, annoyed to be reminded about her lack of friends. "Can't you leave us alone now?"

"No," Silver said, clutching her more firmly. "I'm seeing you back to Skittle Street. Keep together, boys!"

Caydon and Oz, walking ahead of them, reluctantly slowed down.

Lily said, "We don't need you any more."

"I'll be the judge of that," said Silver.

"So I'm stuck with you?"

"'Fraid so. I'm coming to tea."

"What! Who asked you?"

"You did," Silver said, maddeningly cool and professional. "I'm your new best friend."

"No, you're not." Lily was now so annoyed that she didn't care about being polite. "As you've noticed, I don't actually have a best friend. I'm so glad me being a misfit is helpful."

"I didn't say you were a misfit."

"Look, Silver Baggins – or whatever your name is – I'll put up with you at school, but that's the limit. I'm not having you hanging about at home. Don't you have a home of your own to go to?"

They were walking into Plum Terrace, the street around the corner from Skittle Street. "As a matter of fact," Silver said, "I live right here. We've just moved into the purple house at the end of the row. The one with a big peace sign on the door."

"The hippy house! I thought it was empty."

"Me and my parents were flown in last night. It belongs to the SMU."

Silver slowed down as they came to the purple building. Lily had always thought this empty, half-ruined house was a spooky, depressing place. She was startled to see that it had changed. It was still scruffy, but the old oil drum in the front garden was now filled with cheery red geraniums, and there was an air of friendliness.

"This looks – different."

"My mother has a talent for setting up home in a

hurry," Silver said. "And this is a nice house. Our work for the undead unit of the SMU takes us all over the world. Our last posting was literally in the Arctic."

She tightened her grip on Lily's arm and hurried to catch up with Oz and Caydon, who had got ahead again. "Boys – don't turn the corner without me!"

The boys halted. Silver, still gripping Lily, put her head round the corner of Skittle Street and stared down it for ages.

"There're more ghosts than there were this morning," Oz said. "Are you sure normal people can't see them?"

The armed ghosts sent by J made Skittle Street look very odd. They were ghosts of soldiers, in all kinds of uniforms: soldiers in red coats and white gaiters; First World War soldiers in khaki; a group of Roundheads from the Civil War and one Roman centurion. They sat on walls, windowsills and doorsteps, and even walked on the roofs of parked cars. But the few normal, non-magic people on the street didn't seem to notice.

"OK, it looks safe," Silver said. "Let's go." A group of Roundheads stepped back to let them pass.

"You really don't have to come with us."

"Lily, please don't tell me how to do my job."

Just as they were walking down the street, through the strange crowd of ghostly soldiers, Mum came out of Number 18, with baby Daisy in her arms.

"Hi!" she called. "I'm popping to the shop for some

milk." She waited while the three kids and Silver caught up with her. "Here, Lily, take Daisy for a moment," she said as they reached the supermarket.

"OK." Lily shook off Silver's hand and held out her arms for the adorable, pink, plump, sleepy baby. Mum hurried into the shop.

"She's gorgeous," Silver said. "You're so lucky. I've always wanted a baby sister."

They leaned with their backs on the supermarket window and looked out across the street. There was a row of stunted trees on the pavement outside the flats, their branches stirring in the October breeze.

That's funny, Lily thought idly. *I'm sure that tree across the road didn't have any leaves this morning. And I don't remember that branch being so long.*

The longest branch − suddenly covered with fresh green leaves − was growing.

Silver let out a scream. "NO-O-O-O!"

"Silver? What's the matter?"

The branch was reaching rapidly across the road like a leafy snake. It knocked the ghostly soldiers aside, wrapped itself round Daisy − and snatched her out of Lily's arms. At the same time, another branch shot out and lashed Silver to the nearby lamp post.

"DAISY!" Lily shrieked.

Oz and Caydon dashed to the tree and, grasping at it with hands and feet, they tried to climb. Two more branches wound around their arms and legs and whisked them high into the air. The soldiers fired their ghostly guns, but the ghostly bullets bounced straight off the tree back at them.

Silver was deathly pale and looked as if she was almost fainting, but she managed to gasp: "Ring – my – bell!"

"What?"

"Lily – before they get you – ring my bell!"

Lily looked at the grimy bell around Silver's neck, almost hidden under the leaves. She reached over and shook it frantically.

CLANG! CLANG! CLANG!

The little bell pealed out across Holloway like the great bell of a cathedral, loud enough to crack the sky.

Lily, beside herself with terror, clamped her hands over her ears. Suddenly something came roaring out of the sky. She thought at first that it was a witch on a broomstick, and then her heart gave a leap of hope. "Elvira!"

It was Caydon's gran, in her midwife's uniform, not riding a broom but a plastic mop. She landed on the pavement next to Lily and Silver. With a face of thunder, she mumbled a few words and held out her arms. The branches meekly bent down to give her baby Daisy, lowered Oz and Caydon back to the ground, and shrank back into an ordinary tree.

Silver's face was white. "It was my fault," she said

breathlessly. "I didn't think of scanning the trees — I haven't goofed like this since about 1870."

Elvira dropped a kiss on Daisy's head and gave her back to Lily. She patted Silver's shoulder. "Don't you worry, darling. You rang the bell just in time."

"That was Lily." Silver smiled at her. "Thanks for understanding when I burbled at you like an idiot."

She was less cool and professional now, and more like a shaken eleven-year-old. Lily smiled back. "I'm glad you didn't leave us when I was telling you to go away. If you hadn't been here—" This was too dreadful even to think about. Lily shivered and cuddled her baby sister closer. "What was that thing, anyway?"

"Dryads," Elvira said. "Tree spirits. I didn't know Alba had them on her payroll."

In a small voice, Silver asked, "Will you report this?"

"You know I have to, but nobody's going to blame you. Who'd have thought it? There hasn't been any dryad activity in north London since the days when there was a Roman temple on Seven Sisters Road. The SMU will need to take samples from these trees and make them spirit-proof."

"Are they safe now?" Lily asked. "Suppose the branches come to life again and get into our bedrooms?"

"They won't," Elvira said firmly. "Not after the curse I put on those dryads! They're just normal trees now."

"That was incredible," Oz said. "On the pavement one

minute – on the roof the next!"

"I saw right into my bedroom," Caydon said. "It looks tidier from the outside."

Elvira chuckled and gave him a quick hug. "I must get back to the hospital. See you!" She was a magnificent sight as she soared away on her mop into the clouds.

"I didn't know Gran did curses," Caydon said. "I wish I could put a curse on Mr Hepton before my project's due in."

"I got some chocolate biscuits." Mum came out of the shop, with absolutely no idea her baby had nearly been snatched by a tree. "Who's this?" she asked, looking at Silver.

Lily suddenly felt sorry for their pale, crestfallen bodyguard. "This is Silver, from our class. Is it OK if she comes to tea?"

8

The Cursed Bird

Lily took Silver to her bedroom at the top of the tall house. While they were climbing the stairs, they suddenly heard screams coming from the wallpaper roses.

"That might be because of me," Silver said. "Some magic things go crazy when they smell a vampire."

The high-pitched squeals grew louder as they approached the bedroom. Lily opened the door – and gasped. "What's going on?"

Three of the walls were now plain, blank white. The roses were huddled together on the fourth wall in a mish-mash of painted yellow petals.

"I'm sorry," Lily said. "I didn't know they were narrow-minded." She took Silver's hand. "This is Silver and she's a friend of mine who's here to protect us — OK?"

A babble of little voices whined, "Vampire — she's a vampire—"

"So? What could a vampire do to a painted flower? Get back in your places and stop being silly!"

Slowly, rather sulkily, the yellow roses moved back to their proper places on the wallpaper.

"And ABOUT TIME," mewed a familiar voice. "You promised you'd give my fur a deep conditioning treatment! Where have you been?"

Silver gaped at Demerara, who was lying on the bed. "You're — you're the talking cat!"

"Yes, dear," Demerara said graciously, "but you mustn't be frightened of me."

Silver burst out laughing. "That's amazing — she really talks!"

"And what's so funny about a cat talking?" Demerara snapped.

"It's great to meet you," Silver said. "You're a legend."

"A legend, eh?" The golden cat smirked, and stopped being offended. "Well, I suppose I am rather famous in SMU circles."

"My mum would love to meet you too — could you come round some time?"

"I'd love to, dear. Tell her I'm very fond of minced raw chicken. Now if you'll excuse me, I'm about to start my beauty treatment. Perhaps you'd like to help? You don't shampoo an ordinary cat, of course. But there's nothing ORDINARY about me!"

Silver was already Demerara's adoring slave. She was delighted to help Lily shampoo the bossy cat in the bath. They rubbed conditioner into the golden fur, hosed it off with the shower head and then went back to the bedroom to dry her with the hairdryer. The two girls were soon covered with blobs of foam and weak with giggling – the podgy cat's beauty treatment seemed much funnier when there was someone to laugh with.

"Lily," Silver said, gently fluffing the fur around Demerara's neck, "when I said you didn't have a best friend, I wasn't calling you a misfit. It's just that I know how lonely life can be for magic types like us. I haven't had a proper friend for more than two hundred years."

"Nobody at school knows about my magic," Lily said. "But they still think I'm weird."

"Oh, you're not that weird. You should try being a vampire. It's just impossible for us to get close to people. You move into a place, you think the neighbours are really nice – and the next thing you know, they're coming round after dark with lighted sticks. I've lost count of all the homes we've been hounded out of."

"But that was in history, when vampires still bit people," Lily pointed out. "Isn't it easier now you've been sort of cured?"

"Yes. And since the treatment, me and my parents have been working for the SMU," Silver said. "We move around more than ever. But I'm glad we came here." She smiled, a little shyly. "Holloway's a lot nicer than the Arctic."

"Why were you in the Arctic?"

"We were guarding something secret. I'm not allowed to give you any details."

"Do you know how long you'll be staying here?"

Silver shrugged. "It could be days, or months. We never know for certain."

"I wouldn't like the Arctic," Demerara announced. "Snow makes me sneeze, and I don't think igloos look very cosy."

"We didn't live in an igloo." The vampire girl stared wistfully around the comfortable and extremely tidy bedroom (Lily couldn't sleep if something was out of place). "We had a flat in a research station. It wasn't nearly as nice as this."

Once again Lily felt sorry for Silver, with her strange and lonely life. "How did you turn into a vampire, anyway? Did you know the person who bit you?"

"Yes," Silver said. "It was my Auntie Fanny. She came down from Grantham for a visit, and there was a vampire on the stagecoach. By the time she got to our house she was a full-blown vampire herself, and she bit us all the same evening. My mother says she should've known something was wrong when Fanny didn't touch her dinner."

"But that's awful!" Lily couldn't imagine how she'd feel if Mum's sister Lucy turned them all into the undead during one of her visits. "Your parents must've been furious."

Silver smiled. "Yes, at first – but it really wasn't Fanny's fault. We still send her Christmas cards."

"How does it feel? I mean, after the bite?" Lily added. "If you don't mind talking about it."

"I don't mind."

"Did the bite hurt?"

"Yes," Silver said. "But then it feels like you're being sucked out of your own body and spat back into it. And until the treatment, vampires couldn't eat. Now we eat more or less normally. But we still don't bleed."

"What do you mean?"

"It's one of the things that makes me such a good bodyguard. If you cut me or shoot me there isn't any blood and my skin just sort of closes up, a bit like Blu-tack. Caydon's right – I can only be destroyed by a wooden stake driven through my heart."

"Yuck!" Lily stared at Silver's white skin in fascination. "Then what happens?"

"I'd turn to dust."

"Kids!" Mum called from downstairs. "Tea's ready!"

"Don't eat anything till I've tested it." Silver stood up,

giving Demerara one last stroke. "I'm not taking any more chances." She smiled at Lily. "Can I do this again? The beauty treatment, I mean. I haven't had so much fun literally for years."

Over the next couple of days, Silver stuck close to Lily, Oz and Caydon, and Lily found that she was starting to enjoy the company of her bodyguard. For one thing, she was a huge help in class, and polished off Lily's homework in a few minutes.

"I've put in a couple of mistakes," she told Lily, "and I made my writing look like yours. Ms Shah will never notice."

"Are you sure you don't mind?" Lily hated doing homework.

"Of course not – it's a piece of cake. You get very good at school stuff when you've been doing it for more than two hundred years."

"You must be brilliant at passing exams."

"Yes," Silver said, "I've passed thousands of exams. And you know what? They're not nearly as useful as they're made out to be. But that might be because I never get older than eleven and vampires don't really need qualifications."

The boys also found they were getting used to their bodyguard surprisingly quickly.

"It's funny," Oz said, "Mum and Dad are acting as if

Silver totally belongs here – and I catch myself thinking it too."

"She finished my project," Caydon said. "I love her."

Only one thing slightly worried Oz and Lily. On Saturday they had their lessons with Dr Spatz and Greta. Silver wanted to go with them – but they hadn't told her what they had seen there last time. In fact, they hadn't told anyone, even Caydon.

Oz tried to talk Silver out of coming with them. "Dr Spatz and Greta are paid by the SMU so we won't need you. Maybe you'd better stay here and guard Caydon."

"Caydon doesn't need guarding," Silver said. "He's at the church bazaar this afternoon, helping Elvira with her food stall. He couldn't be safer – she's the best witch in north London."

"There's no need to tell Silver anything," Lily said, when the twins were in private again. "It'll probably be normal this time."

Dad had dropped Oz, Lily and Silver at the Spatzes' house in Gospel Oak. Halfway up the path to the front door, they were suddenly overwhelmed by a stink so foul and so dreadful that Silver turned white as a sheet and Lily threw up beside the dustbin.

"Wow," choked Oz. "That's like the worst fart in history! It must be the drains!"

Silver pulled her scuffed plastic meter from her backpack.

She shuddered over the reading. "This isn't just the smell of drains – it's the stench of pure EVIL!" She began to scrabble for something in the backpack. "OK, I don't have time to get authorization – cover your noses and mouths—"

She produced a tiny red spray can and squirted out a sparkling jet of light. When it hit the house, there was a great hissing and a cloud of steam. Once this had cleared, the deathly smell was gone. The front garden smelt of normal London air again.

Lily dared to take a couple of deep breaths and stopped feeling sick. "Ugh, that was disgusting! Is it OK now?"

"No," Silver said grimly. "Something serious has happened here. I'd better call for backup."

She took her phone from one rainbow sleeve and quickly sent a text. Then she rang the doorbell and hammered the knocker. "OPEN UP!"

Far away, somewhere inside the flat, they heard a long, thin wail.

"Greta!" Lily called through the letter box. "Don't be scared – it's only us! We've come for our lessons!"

There was a long silence and then the sound of shuffling footsteps in the hall. The front door opened just wide enough for Greta to poke her nose through the crack. "Lily? Oh – who's the vampire?"

Silver showed her SMU card. "I'm from the Nosferatu bodyguard unit. Let us in, please – and don't try to escape."

She pushed her way into the flat. Greta stood aside helplessly. Her long grey hair was a mess – half of it had been burned off, and her black velvet dress was a charred rag.

"Don't touch her!" warned Silver.

Lily ignored her and put her arms around the weeping, shaking minor witch. "It's OK, Silver's on our side and she's really nice. What happened?"

Oz asked, "Is Dr Spatz here?"

Greta blew her nose on a large, dirty purple handkerchief. "No," she said shakily. "They took Daddy away."

"Who took him?"

"Some horrible people – from D33."

"But what would D33 want with an old violin teacher?"

"Dr Spatz must be more than just an old violin teacher," Silver said. "D33 doesn't kidnap people by mistake."

"Well, this must be a mistake." Greta hid her face in the handkerchief. "Daddy doesn't have any special powers! He's completely ordinary! Isn't he, Oz?"

"Yes," Oz said, avoiding Lily's eye.

Silver sighed impatiently. "There's a terrible stink of LIES in here! Don't any of you see what we're up against?"

"Hey!" Oz yelped suddenly. "I've remembered who that bloke was – the photo on Dr Spatz's phone! I've seen him before because he's on the cover of my music book. It was Johannes Brahms!"

"But —" Lily did not know a lot about Oz's music "— he's dead, isn't he?"

"He's been dead for more than a hundred years, so Dr Spatz must've found a way to travel back in time!"

"OK," Silver said. "Greta Prunella Lavinia Spatz, I'm arresting you on a charge of illegal tampering with the time stream." She frowned at Lily. "And I ought to arrest you two for keeping quiet about it." She seemed hurt as well as angry.

"Sorry we didn't tell you," Lily said. "But we didn't want to get them into trouble."

"And we didn't have proof," Oz added. "Not till I recognized Brahms."

"Have you told Caydon?"

"No, he doesn't know either."

Silver's face softened. "I suppose you meant well. But you'd better bring me up to speed before the SWAT team gets here."

Led by a snivelling Greta, they moved down the corridor to the kitchen. Silver made mugs of tea, while the twins reported everything they had seen.

"Daddy's not a wicked man!" Greta pleaded. "He only wanted to meet his favourite composers!"

Silver asked, "Do you have his phone?"

Greta nodded miserably and took her father's phone from the pocket of her charred dress. Silver opened the photo file and found the picture of plump, bearded

Brahms with Dr Spatz. It was odd to see this famous genius looking just like a normal old man, grinning from ear to ear. Silver quickly flicked through the other pictures. They were all of Dr Spatz posing with famous composers – Haydn, Beethoven, Bach, Vivaldi, Mendelssohn. The only one Lily recognized was Mozart, a laughing young man in a white wig, jokily holding his fingers in rabbit ears behind Dr Spatz's head.

"I begged him not to risk it," Greta said. "I might not be very good at magic, but I do know that time travel can be dreadfully dangerous. Every time he went, I worried that he'd never come back. It's almost a relief to have it all out in the open. Do I have time for another cup of tea before I go to prison?"

"Plenty of time." Silver switched on the kettle again. "I stood down the alert. There's a single police car waiting outside now." She was brisk and teacher-like, and suddenly seemed much older.

Greta sniffed. "What will they do with me?"

"Probably nothing serious," Silver said. "If you tell J what you know."

"But – I've told you everything!"

"Come on, Greta! How on earth did a half-baked conjuror like your dad manage to travel back in time?"

"Dr Spatz isn't magic," Oz said. "That's what he told me, anyway."

Greta let out a long sigh, like a deflating balloon. "He

wasn't exactly telling the truth. He had enough magic to mess about with that wretched bird – even though Mummy told him there was a curse on it before she died."

Lily's stomach hadn't been feeling great since she'd thrown up outside, and the mention of the bird made it flutter uncomfortably. She reached blindly across the kitchen table and Oz's hand found hers – he had sensed the danger too.

"OK, Greta spit it out," said Silver, "from the beginning."

"My mother had a beautiful golden phoenix," Greta said. "When she left it to my father, she told him it was made of special chocolate that could make you travel back in time. She said it was a very difficult spell to do, and everyone who owned the phoenix in the past had come to a terribly bad end. She said there was a curse on it. But Daddy wanted to meet all the great composers – and one day he got hold of the right materials to carry out the spell." She blew her long nose again. "I begged him not to. But he said it was the perfect opportunity. So he cut off one of the bird's chocolate legs—"

"The phoenix in Caydon's vision had a wooden leg," Oz remembered.

"I made it a little wooden leg out of cocktail sticks," Greta said. "Poor thing, it looked all lopsided!"

"Wow," said Silver, shaking her head. "You are in such a lot of trouble!"

Greta exploded into a fresh fit of sobbing. Lily let go of Oz's hand to hug her again.

"Don't be mean – anyone can see she's not a criminal."

"Listen to me, Greta." Silver eyed her sternly. "Where's the phoenix now?"

"They took it," Greta gulped. "The horrid people who took Daddy. They bundled him and the phoenix into the broom cupboard and they all disappeared in a ball of fire. The flames didn't hurt me – they just burned off half my hair and my dress and one shoe. Silver, I beg you, please tell them to lock me away in prison, I'll be safe there! I've never been so frightened in my life!" She lowered her voice fearfully. "They couldn't come inside unless I let them in, you see – but I had to let them in. I had no choice."

"Why?" asked Silver.

"Because," Greta whispered, "one of them was – my mother."

9

A Stitch in Time

The shocked silence stretched on for ages, broken only by Greta's soft sobs and the sound of a train rumbling past at the end of the garden.

"Your mother?" Silver's face and lips were white. "What are you talking about? You said your mother was dead!"

"I was lying," Greta said. "She didn't die – she left us. On my thirtieth birthday."

"How horrible," Oz said.

"Actually, it was quite a relief. She never liked me. I could never be magic enough to please her. She tried to teach me spells and when I got them wrong, she used to hit my ears with a ruler."

"She sounds really mean." Lily was fond of Greta, and it was awful to see how sad she was.

"But I'm nothing like her – please believe me, Lily! I'm not wicked, and neither is Daddy!"

"I believe you." -

"Me too," Oz said kindly. "It's not your fault."

Greta looked at Silver. "I don't care what you do to me – but you have to save him! My aunt wants to go back in time and she thinks she's found a time stitch. She can't make the chocolate work for her – so when she found out that Daddy had been time-hopping she ordered Mummy to kidnap him. They'll torture him to get at his secret!"

Lily was confused. "Your aunt?"

"Alba."

"Who?"

"Don't you remember?" Oz said. "Alba is the oldest of those thirty-three wicked daughters – the one Albion was named after. She's the head of D33."

"Yes." Greta hung her head. "She's also my aunt."

"WHAT?" gasped Silver. "You mean – your mother is one of the original sisters?"

"Yes. Many of them married mortals. Her undercover mortal name was Mrs Sheila Spatz, but her real name is Duodecima – Daddy used to call her 'Twelvey'."

Silver sat down heavily. "Oh, bum. What am I meant to do next?" She was almost talking to herself. "This is serious. If I mess up this time. . . I think I'd better turn this one over to my commanding officer." She pulled her phone out of her sleeve and quickly sent a text. "OK, we'll go out to the car. Stick close together."

"So you're taking us back to the safe house by the sea?" Oz guessed. "Or the MI6 building?"

"We're going back to Holloway," Silver said. "My commanding officer is my mum."

She hurried them out of the flat and into the police car, and they hurtled to Holloway at breakneck speed with the siren howling. The car stopped round the corner from Skittle Street, outside the purple hippy house where Silver was staying with her parents. Lily noticed that the house had changed again. The front garden had been tidied and swept, and the front door had been repainted dark blue with a pattern of gold stars.

"Phew!" Silver said. "I was terrified we'd get ambushed on the way here. I had ghastly visions of you all being killed, and me getting demoted to Pixie Patrol." She let them into the hall. "Mum!"

A woman's voice called, "In the kitchen, darling!"

Lily and Oz looked round curiously. The hall of the hippy house was scuffed and shabby, and an orange bicycle leaned against the dark purple wall. There was a strong smell of joss sticks.

As Silver led them down the hall to the kitchen, a high, mewing voice floated towards them. "My back fur was smooth but Lily did my tail in beautiful curls, and I was trying a rather fabulous burgundy claw polish. . ."

Demerara was sitting in queenly state in the middle of the kitchen table, a bowl of minced chicken before her. "Ah, here are the children now. Hello, dears."

"G—good gracious!" Greta goggled at her in amazement. "It spoke!"

The cat's emerald eyes narrowed crossly. "You must be Greta. I don't think much of your hairstyle."

"It's not on purpose," Lily said. "Her hair got burnt off."

"Oh, you poor thing!" Demerara stopped looking cross. "That happened to me once, my dear, I was as bald as a sausage! I know just how you feel."

"Welcome to our temporary home," Silver's mother said. "Sit down here, Greta. Well done for bringing them, darling. That was very quick thinking."

Silver dropped her backpack. "I didn't want to mess up again, like I did with the dryads."

"You can relax now. This house is completely caged." Silver's mum smiled at Oz and Lily. "That means it's been sealed against bad magic." She was a youngish woman, about the same age as Emily Spoffard, and her old jeans and jersey were splattered with white paint. "I'm in the middle of redecorating Silver's bedroom" she explained. "I never can settle in a place until I've made it homelike."

The kitchen was a cosy, cluttered cave. The sink was cracked, the stove looked as if it had come off a skip and the fridge was on its last legs, but Lily decided she liked this room. It was in perfect order, with all the cups in neat rows and the plates in tidy piles. There were cheery strings of pink fairy lights, which she loved. Dad would only let her have a few in her bedroom, because he was worried they would burn the house down.

"You've done it really well," she said. "This place was a ruin just a few days ago."

"I've had over two hundred years of practice," Silver's mum said, laughing (which made her look just like her daughter). "In my time I've done igloos in the Arctic, mud huts in Africa and medieval castles in Transylvania — compared to which a place like this is a doddle. I'm Cathy, by the way, and this is Vaz."

"Hi, guys." In the corner was a man with a straggling brown beard, knitting a long orange scarf. He was wearing a shapeless rainbow jersey, like Silver's. "Make yourselves at home. Have some nettle juice."

"Shuddup, Dad," Silver said. "They don't want that green sludge."

"Full of iron," her dad said. "Really healthy for us vampires. Great for our bowels too."

"Dad!"

"Since the new treatment, we often find it very difficult to poo."

"Dad, I haven't brought friends home for about sixty years. Could you please stop embarrassing me?" She rolled her eyes at Oz and Lily. "Sorry."

"Yes, spare us the lecture about poo and make yourself useful," Cathy said. "Go and prepare the transporter."

"I've done it." Vaz started another row of knitting. "No need to hassle me. I lit some scented candles too."

"Did you unlock the docking portal?"

"Oh, man – I knew there was something I forgot." He put down his knitting and slowly stood up. "I suppose I'd better do it now." He shuffled out of the room.

"I wish he'd finish his hippy phase," Silver said. "Doesn't he know the 1960s are over?"

"Now, don't start on about that again," her mother said briskly. "The useless hippy act is a very good cover."

"Huh. I wish it *was* an act!" Silver muttered. "I'm over two hundred and I still have to wear my dad's rubbish knitting!"

"Never mind, dear," Demerara purred kindly. "I like nice bright colours."

Cathy patted her head. "Thanks so much for popping round, Demerara. It's been thrilling to meet you. But I think you ought to go back to Skittle Street now."

The cat's furry face pleated into a scowl. "I can't. I popped round to your house because Spike threw me out."

"Threw you out?" Oz chuckled. "You must've done something pretty serious!"

"It's a silly fuss about nothing," Demerara hissed.

96

"The drain was swarming with his horrible, badly behaved rat army. I lost my temper and killed a couple of them."

"That was really naughty," Lily said. "Spike's army is there to guard Daisy."

"But I'm a cat! It's in my nature to kill rats. I tried to explain this to Spike, but he was too angry to listen."

"That doesn't sound like Spike," Oz said. "How many did you kill?"

"I told you — just one or two." Demerara shrugged. "Or eighteen."

"Eighteen! That must've been a bloodbath!"

"It wasn't pretty."

"Yuck," Lily said, with a shudder. "No wonder Spike was angry with you."

"I've never seen him so furious — I won't tell you the awful names he called me. I decided to stay here until he calms down and stops trying to bite my bum."

"Well, OK," Cathy said. "You can stay here for a bit. It's nice to have a cat around again, isn't it, Silver? Ordinary mortal cats run away from vampires."

"Before we got bitten we had a very sweet cat called Tibby," Silver said sadly. "She went to live with the school teacher and never let me stroke her again."

Lily had another moment of feeling sorry for her. As if being turned into a vampire wasn't bad enough, she'd also lost her beloved pet.

Vaz came back into the kitchen. "All ready for her now."

"I know you've been preparing a torture chamber," Greta said. "But you don't need to torture me. I'll tell you everything."

"Nobody's getting tortured," Cathy assured her. "J will ask you a few questions, and then you'll go off to prison via the secret underground emergency network — we have a portal in the cellar. And you'll only be locked up to keep you safe from your mother and aunts."

"What about Daddy?"

"Hey, take a chill pill," Vaz said, picking up his knitting. "All the top agents will be looking for him. Have some cobweb tea to calm you down."

"Don't," Silver said. "It's disgusting."

Down the hall, the front door slammed. "That'll be J," said Cathy.

The elegant man known as J came into the cluttered hippy kitchen and sat down as if he'd known it all his life. "Well, I didn't see this one coming. That was very nice work, Silver."

"Thank you, sir." Silver looked older again, standing to attention.

J glanced over at her dad. "Hello, Vaz. Nice knitting."

"It's a scarf," Vaz said. "It's going to be your Christmas present."

"How kind." J turned to Demerara. "I've had a

complaint about you. Spike says you've been on a killing spree."

"Only rats," Demerara said. "No need to make a fuss."

"He says they were some of his best officers."

"How was I to know?" The cat tossed her little head. "They weren't exactly wearing uniforms."

"Please. . ." Greta blurted out, "do you know where they've taken Daddy?"

Lily was glad to see that J's face was kind. "Sorry, not yet," he said. "But you can help us, Greta. How much do you know about this time stitch?"

"Excuse me – but what is a time stitch?" Oz had been longing to ask this question.

"Time is like this piece of knitting," Vaz said, holding up his boggled orange scarf. "See this hole?" He stuck a finger through it. "This is where I dropped a stitch. When there's a dropped stitch in the fabric of time, it makes a hole. And that makes it a perfect entry point for time travel."

"When we know about a time stitch," J said, "we can guard it. The trouble is, we don't know about all the holes. Dr Spatz must've found a new one."

"Oh, yes," Greta said, "but I don't know where it is – honestly! All I know is that once he got through the dropped stitch, he could travel in time wherever he wanted."

J was stern now. "But that's not the whole story, is it?

Your father doesn't have enough magic to do it on his own."

Greta looked down at her hands. Lily could see she was frightened. "It was the chocolate phoenix. You'll find the rest of the leg we cut off in our kitchen drawer, wrapped in clingfilm."

"Thank you, we've already got it," J said. "But it's not much good by itself. What else did he use?"

Once more Greta started to cry. "Please forgive me, Lily. Forgive me, Oz. He swore it wouldn't do any harm!"

The twins looked at each other. Ever since they were babies they had heard another voice in their heads as if they were three instead of two. Nowadays it seemed to come from Daisy, and at this moment they felt her sense of looming danger.

"It was when you started coming to us for lessons," Greta said. "Daddy heard all about your special powers and guessed you were carriers of the rare D33 gene. So he – he stole a little bit of your DNA."

Oz shivered. "How? Why didn't I notice? Was he doing it while I was playing the violin?"

"All he needed was one hair from each of you, and one from Caydon. That's why he invited Caydon to tea that time." Greta blew her nose loudly. "You three, you see – you're all descended from the two of my aunts who turned good. That's why your powers are so special. Daddy only had to melt together a tiny scrap of hair and a crumb of magic chocolate, and off he could go to meet his favourite composers. He was saving the last bit for a long lunch with Sir Edward Elgar. Oh, Lily, please say you forgive me!"

"Of course I do!" Lily jumped up from her chair to give her another hug. It was rather creepy to think of Dr Spatz stealing their DNA, but Greta was so miserable that it was impossible not to feel sorry for her. "None of this is your fault."

J sighed. "No, you didn't mean any harm. But I need more about this dropped stitch in time. Did your mother or your father tell you where – or rather, when – it was?"

Greta said, "Mummy told me that a great fire burned a hole in the time fabric."

"Fire! That ties in with Caydon's visions! Think carefully, Greta – did she say anything else?"

"Just family news," Greta said. "My Auntie Alba's been to parenting classes. Now she wants to build relationships with all her children."

10

Prediction

"Deep!" Caydon said, when Oz and Lily had told him everything. "Your Saturday sounds loads more interesting than mine. I spent the whole afternoon at the church bazaar, cooking burgers on Gran's stall. And then I went to see my dad and we watched football. The next thing I know I'm being dragged out of bed at dawn and bundled off in a helicopter. I wish someone would explain what's going on. My mum thinks I'm on a trip to the National Gallery."

It was Sunday morning, and the helicopter had been waiting in the car park behind Waitrose on Holloway Road. Caydon, Oz and Lily – guarded by Silver, who was openly carrying a machine gun – were being whisked away to a mystery destination.

"I had to get you early," Silver said. "Before you went off to church." Caydon was an altar boy at St Benedict's in Pooter Street. "I can't go inside your church."

"Of course – because you're a vampire," Caydon said. "Is it true that you scream when someone holds up a cross?"

"No," Silver said stiffly. "That's just in films. I can't enter St Benedict's because of the gargoyles."

"What's a gargoyle?" asked Lily.

"It's an ugly little stone monster," Silver said. "You find them carved on ancient churches. In the olden days, people thought they kept off evil spirits. St Benedict's is a Victorian church, but medieval stuff was fashionable then, so the architect put gargoyles on it. And every time I walk down Pooter Street they scream at me."

"Really? Our gargoyles?" Caydon was delighted. "That's so cool – I wish I could hear them!"

Silver frowned. "Take it from me, you're lucky you can't."

"But you're not an evil spirit," Lily said. "That's so unfair."

"Gargoyles haven't moved with the times," Silver said. "They're like the roses on your wallpaper – hardwired to scream the place down whenever they smell a vampire. It takes a very long time for that kind of prejudice to die out."

"So is it just screeching?" Caydon asked. "Or do they say things?"

"Look, shuddup! Can't you see she doesn't like talking about it?" said Lily.

"Shuddup yourself! I've got a right to ask questions about my own church."

"It's not a joke, you know – why can't you ever take anything seriously?"

"Why can't you lighten up sometimes?"

"I wish you'd both shut up," Oz said. "I want to know about Alba. Why was J so shocked when he heard about the parenting classes? How many kids has she got?"

"More than two hundred," Silver said. "And she's never cared about them before now."

"Are they all dead? Is that why she needs to go back in time to find them?"

"I don't know any more than you do." Silver stopped looking sad and turned businesslike. "My orders are simply to deliver you to the local SMU agent."

"Local where?"

"You'll see – we're nearly there."

The windowless helicopter landed and Silver opened the door. The chilly air that gusted in smelt of the sea, but they were not back at the safe house. This was another car park, behind a branch of Argos.

"Stick close together," Silver said, clutching the gun under her duffel coat.

She led them out of the car park, down a narrow alley, and on to a wide, windy street beside a choppy grey sea.

"Hey – we're at the seaside!" Caydon cried. "I've never seen so many amusement arcades and chip shops!"

"Welcome to Blackpool," Silver said. "This is called the Golden Mile."

The beach was enormous, and the seafront seemed to stretch away into infinity. It was a blustery day in late October and the only people on the sand were a couple of men with dogs. Most of the shops along the endless promenade were shut up for the winter. Silver took them into a pub on a corner. It was almost empty. She nodded to the woman behind the bar and they went through a door with a sign that said, KIDS ROOM – SOFT PLAY AND TRAMPOLINES. There were no little children playing here. The only person in the room was an old man with grey hair, in a brown raincoat.

Silver saluted and showed him her SMU card. "Good morning, sir. I've brought the Spoffard twins and Caydon Campbell."

The man showed them his own SMU card. "Hi, kids. I'm Chief Inspector Roy Parkin – officially retired, but I deal with all the unexplained business round here." He shook hands with them all. "No time to hang about, I'm afraid. You're about to assist at a future-casting. That means you'll be meeting someone with a gift for seeing pictures of a possible future – things that *might* happen – that *will* happen unless something is done—"

"My gran does that," Caydon said.

"So you're Elvira's lad? We did our National Service in magic together. Is she well?"

"Yes, thanks."

"Well, this future-caster is even better than your gran. She's called Madge Fladgate, and between ourselves she's a bit of an old so-and-so. You're not to worry if she doesn't cooperate at first."

Caydon groaned loudly. "Mrs Fladgate! I remember her from the SMU safe house – she hates me!"

"He bumped into her on a skateboard and she was really angry," Lily said. "After that, every time she saw him she told him all the horrible things she saw in his future. Things like going bald."

"She's a nasty old bag," Caydon said crossly. "I'll stay outside if you don't mind."

The Chief Inspector chuckled, but shook his head. "Oh, no, we can't do it without you."

"OK, but keep her as far away from me as possible."

They left the pub by a side door and followed the policeman past a row of small shops, all shut up for the winter, except one on the end. In its narrow window was a large painting of a beautiful young gypsy woman with black hair and scarlet lips, bending over a crystal ball. Underneath was written:

"Huh," Caydon said, "if she really looked like that I wouldn't mind so much."

Chief Inspector Parkin pushed open the creaking door and they walked into a small, stuffy room hung with black curtains. A wrinkled old woman with mad white hair was sitting behind a table with a crystal ball on it, reading a magazine.

She scowled when she saw the inspector. "Bog off, policeman – I don't like snoopers," she snarled.

Parkin smiled, and pulled aside one of the black curtains to reveal a pile of cardboard boxes full of shampoo. "Not surprising, when you're still receiving stolen goods!"

"I don't know what you're talking about. Can't a woman buy a bottle of shampoo?"

The chief inspector sat down. "Relax, I haven't come to arrest you. And I might not tell my police friends where I found all this stolen stuff – if you'll do a little job for the government."

"I told you," said Mrs Fladgate, "I've done enough for the SMU." She looked at Oz, Lily and Caydon, and her wrinkled lips stretched into a smile. "Well, well – you've brought the three gene carriers! Here's the girl who doesn't know how to use her own magic. Here's her genius twin brother, who'll grow up to be a famous violin player. Here's the CHEEKY boy with the skateboard. Plus a dear little vampire!"

"Stop it, Madge," Chief Inspector Parkin said calmly. "I've brought them to help you get a picture of what D33 is planning for the future. Silver's their bodyguard. So don't try anything funny."

Caydon nudged Oz. "Hey, she says you're going to be famous!"

"That's just rubbish." Oz's face was hot. It embarrassed him to talk about his music.

"My predictions are not rubbish, young man," Mrs Fladgate snapped. "I know who you are! You're the three carriers – though you're nothing without that sister of yours."

"Daisy?" Lily was alarmed. "She's only a baby! She's – she's too little to be mixed up in all this!"

Mrs Fladgate cackled like an old witch. "Daisy is the little walnut tree in the middle of the grove."

"What're you talking about?" Lily suddenly wanted to be at home, to guard her sister.

"Ignore her," the chief inspector said. "She's trying to distract you. Come on, Madge. Put that silly crystal ball away. You know it doesn't work."

"The customers like it," Mrs Fladgate said sulkily. "It doesn't work, but so what? They never want to know what's REALLY going to happen to them. All right, tell the carriers to sit down, and I'll fetch a projecting screen."

She tottered off behind one of the black curtains, and came out a moment later with a yellow plastic washing-up bowl, which she placed in the middle of the table. There was about a centimetre of water sloshing around at the bottom. Lily, Oz and Caydon sat down. Mrs Fladgate took the chair between Lily and Oz.

"Join hands and look hard at the water in this bowl."

They all joined hands around the table. Lily took Mrs Fladgate's hand, which felt like a cold claw. It was like being part of a machine that had slotted into place, she thought. A charge of magic energy shot through the circle.

"OW!" Mrs Fladgate groaned. "It's all right for you kids – my old bones can't take this kind of power. Keep looking for a picture of the future."

The three children stared into the bottom of the plastic bowl.

"I can't see a thing," Oz said. "Am I doing it right?"

"Keep still," said the chief inspector. "She's off!"

Oz and Lily gasped as the old fortune-teller's icy fingers closed around theirs. Her bent old body stiffened and shuddered.

Caydon cried out: "Look!"

A single wave passed across the smooth water, and Oz and Lily saw the picture.

It was like watching a film, yet you could feel the cool breeze blowing off it, and hear sounds of traffic. They were looking at a wide river, in the middle of a strange city. There were gleaming modern office towers and peculiar old bridges with houses on them, and the turrets of an old red-brick castle.

"This looks a bit like London," Oz said. "Except there's no St Paul's and I can't see Big Ben or the Houses of Parliament, or Tower Bridge. And what are all those big black boats?"

"Oh, it's London, all right!" Mrs Fladgate said, with a nasty chuckle. "Those are coffin boats, carrying away the people who've died of the plague."

"When is this?" Oz was confused. They'd had a history lesson about the plague. It had happened hundreds of years ago, when there weren't any cars or office towers.

"Right now! Someone's been mucking about with the past and it's all come out different. There isn't any Parliament now! There's no such thing as a vote!" Mrs Fladgate was wild-eyed with excitement. "It's the cruel reign of King Brian. He encourages the plague to keep the population down. Football matches are banned. The television's really boring!"

The picture of this dreadful alternative London dissolved. Mrs Fladgate suddenly flopped forward into the plastic bowl like a puppet whose strings had been cut.

For several minutes they all sat in shocked silence.

Caydon whispered, "Is she dead or something?"

"Certainly NOT!" Mrs Fladgate sat bolt upright. "I haven't even started! I know something DREADFUL about your future, young man!"

"Here we go," Caydon said crossly. "Now she's going to tell me about getting fat or bald or something. Well, I don't care."

"Oh, you'll care about this!" Cackling nastily, Mrs Fladgate stood up and shuffled round the table to whisper in Caydon's ear. Whatever it was that she whispered, Caydon was horrified. He jumped up with a strangled shout of "NO!" and bolted out of the shop.

"Caydon!" Oz tried to run after him, but the chief inspector took his arm to stop him.

"No need to panic, Oz."

"But this must be something REALLY bad!"

"Nonsense! Madge might be good at future-casting and what-iffing, but she's only average at fortune-telling. She doesn't have clearance for any serious stuff."

The mean old woman scowled. "I can see further than you think, policeman! Now leave me alone."

They left Mrs Fladgate's stuffy little shop and found Caydon across the road, gazing at the sea, stunned and trembling.

Silver said, "You'd better tell us what she said."

"No way!" Caydon snapped. "It's a private thing, OK? Just don't ask me!"

"It's obviously something embarrassing," Lily said. "But you can't keep it to yourself."

"Yes, I can – I'm NEVER telling anyone. And anyway, I'm going to make sure it doesn't come true – got that?"

"It can't be important," Silver said. "If it is, the department will see it anyway."

"I hope not!" Caydon was seriously rattled. "I don't want anyone to see – and the department doesn't need to know because it's never going to happen!"

Oz was Caydon's best friend, and he was sure he'd find out about the dreadful prediction as soon as the two of them were alone.

But Caydon looked him in the eye and said, very firmly, "I can't even tell you. Please don't ask me. I just wish I'd never got mixed up with magic in the first place!"

11

London Isn't Burning

The return flight was gloomy. Caydon was in a glowering sulk. He snapped at Oz and scowled at Lily.

"I don't care what Mrs Fladgate predicted," Lily said. "You don't have to take it out on the rest of us."

"Leave him alone," Oz said. "Can't you see he's had a shock?"

"So what? Nobody ever cares when I'VE had a shock. He's always getting at me for not being brave – now he's acting like a total wimp."

"Oh, I'm not a wimp," Caydon said darkly. "Considering what I've just heard, I'm being incredibly brave – anybody else would be screaming."

Oz nudged him. "You're not going to die, are you?"

"No. It's worse."

"Shut up, you lot." Silver said. "That means you too, Caydon — I've no idea what that mad old bat said to you, but she doesn't have the power for that sort of prediction. She probably said you'd grow up to be uncool or something. Get over it."

"Not as bad as that," said Caydon, suddenly smiling. "Nothing could make ME uncool."

Oz grinned back at him, relieved that his best friend, and distant cousin, wasn't in serious danger. "Well, I'm certainly not going to be cool when I grow up — not if she was right about me."

"Never mind," said Caydon. "Maybe you'll be the world's first cool violin player."

Lily said, "I want to know what she meant about Daisy. We shouldn't have left her."

"Daisy's fine." Silver leaned across the machine gun on her knee to pat Lily's arm. "She's at my house, with Mum and Elvira. Honestly, she's totally safe."

"What about our parents?"

"They're having lunch at one of the SMU's sealed pubs. Caydon, your mum's gone to a sealed cinema with her two best friends. We're not going back to Skittle Street."

"I'm starving," Caydon said. "Can we have lunch at that pub?"

"Sorry, we're headed for MI6." Silver glanced round at them, with an expression that looked odd on her eleven-year-old face. "I don't know if I should tell you this – but I think we're going on a pretty serious mission."

This pushed old Mrs Fladgate out of their minds. They were all very quiet.

"I haven't been told anything officially," Silver said. "It was the way Mum sounded when I called her. And I could hear Dad shouting 'Love you, baby' in the background. I could tell they were worried about me. They know I'm very experienced – but parents are always parents, even after two hundred and forty-six years."

Oz asked, "What's the mission?"

"Sorry, I don't know. But I do know we're all going to have to work together as a team. We can't afford any more silly squabbles."

The twins and Caydon looked at one another; the power was strong between them, and nobody felt like squabbling.

"Very well done, everyone," J said. "Thanks to you three carriers, Madge's vision was beautifully clear and we think we've found Alba's time stitch. All the signs tell us that she's planning to make her entry on Sunday the second of September 1666. Does that date mean anything to you?"

Oz, Lily and Caydon looked at one another blankly.

"But we saw a modern city," Oz said. "With cars and trains – it didn't look like sixteen – whenever."

"The picture was full of clues," J said. "Do you remember seeing an old castle beside the river, with red-brick turrets? It was called Baynard's Castle and it burned to the ground in 1666 – the date of the Great Fire of London."

They had all heard of the Great Fire of London. Lily and Oz had done a project about it at their last school. "If that castle burned to the ground, why could we see it?" Lily asked.

"Because in Madge's awful vision, it survived," J said. That vision showed what London could look like today – if Alba and her wicked sisters manage to slip through the dropped stitch and put the fire out."

"But –" Lily was puzzled "–wouldn't that be quite a good thing?"

"The Great Fire ended the plague," Oz remembered. "And in that vision there were plague barges."

"Yes," J said, "there was a very bad strain of plague around in those days. It was wiped out when the city was consumed by fire. If there hadn't been a fire, that strain would have got stronger and less possible to cure, and, we estimate, a third of the population would have died of it. That's why you children must make sure that fire starts."

There was a long silence.

"So," Oz said slowly, "you want us to go back in time to sixteen-whatever –"

"1666."

"– and START the Great Fire of London?"

"More or less," J said. "Alba can't stop the fire starting, but you have to make sure she doesn't manage to put it out. If she puts it out, you lot must start it again."

There was an even longer silence.

"I've been with the SMU for more than a hundred years," Silver said, "and this is the craziest job I've ever heard of."

"We're living in crazy times," said J.

They were in his grand secret office in the MI6 building beside the river, and he was wearing the dark blue uniform of a senior officer in the Navy. He stood up behind his desk. "If you agree to this little jaunt back to the seventeenth century, you'll start your training after lunch. If you don't agree," he added, very solemnly, "we could wake up tomorrow morning in a different reality – an evil D33 dictatorship, in the cruel reign of King Brian. Our future-casters tell me that King Brian is just a puppet in the hands of Alba and her sisters." He shook his head sadly. "How does she attain such power? We don't know. But something vitally important will be destroyed, unless that fire takes place."

"It'd be so weird to wake up and find everything different," Caydon said thoughtfully. "Would we know it was different? If history had been changed that long ago, wouldn't we have grown up with King Brian? Wouldn't we just think he was the normal king?"

J smiled. "That's a very good question. I think you'd all notice because you're carriers."

"So we'd just wake up one day and there'd be somebody else on the stamps and the money," Lily said. "And we'd know about it but nobody else would? This is making my brain hurt!"

"Try not to think about it too hard," J said briskly. "You don't need to understand all the details. Your job will be simple – to stop D33 putting out the Great Fire of London. Your power as carriers will be enough to transport Silver as your bodyguard."

"Thank you, sir," Silver said.

Lily said, "I'm glad you'll be there. You know more about things in the past."

There was a knock on the door. Three men, armed with machine guns and dressed in the white clothes and hats of chefs, pushed in three trolleys laden with food.

"First, you must have something to eat," said J. "Food in the past will be full of germs and you mustn't touch it."

The armed chefs quickly set up a table, covered it with a white cloth and set it with plates, knives and forks. The office began to fill with delicious smells.

One of the chefs asked, "Do you need the cat food, sir?"

"Oh, yes, I nearly forgot. Bring in those ridiculous animals."

Two armed policemen came in, each holding a reinforced pet carrier.

"This is the LIMIT!" screeched Demerara, inside one pet carrier. "Let me out! Let me get at that GHASTLY RODENT!"

"Let me out!" squeaked the angry voice of Spike from inside the other carrier. "I'm going to sink my teeth into her FAT BUM!"

"Stop it at once – both of you!" J was very stern, though Lily was sure he was trying not to smile.

She went over to peer through the steel bars of Demerara's pet carrier. "What's going on – have you been arrested again?"

"Lily, he won't stop attacking me!" A pair of angry green eyes glared at her from the depths of the pet carrier. "Spike's the one who should be locked up."

"You both had to be locked up," J said. "You wouldn't stop fighting."

"That OLD BAG killed six more of my best rats!"

"They were INSOLENT LOUTS and they STOLE my lovely piece of pizza!"

"The argument will have to wait," J said, "until this emergency is over. Let me say this to all of you, animals and children. For the sake of this mission, you must forget any silly disagreements and work together as a perfect unit."

They were all silent for a moment.

"I'll stop being angry about that prediction," said Caydon.

"Oh, all right," said Spike. The easy-going rat was always the first to get his temper back. "I won't make any more trouble. I'll put off biting her bum till it's over."

"And I suppose I'll stop killing his army," Demerara hissed. "I'm as patriotic as the next cat and I'm doing this for my country. Now someone kindly give me some FOOD."

One of the policemen unlocked the pet carriers. Demerara climbed out into Lily's arms. Spike dropped to the floor and jumped on to Oz's trainer, and they all sat down to a very good lunch of roast chicken, with trifle for pudding. Demerara ate a saucer of cat food and half the chicken on Lily's plate, and was polite to Spike. They were all talking and laughing normally – but they knew the coming mission was going to be very dangerous, and they sensed it like a gathering storm.

12

Time Travellers

"I thought we'd just jump straight back." Lily rubbed her sore arm crossly. "I didn't know we'd have to do all this other stuff first. And that injection really hurt."

Preparing for time travel turned out to be complicated. After lunch, Oz, Caydon and Lily had been given painful injections for smallpox and bubonic plague. They were then taken to a professor at the Victoria and Albert Museum, who fitted them with real seventeenth-century clothes (the SMU time scientists said anything modern would simply disappear in the past). Silver hadn't needed the injections, but she joined them for this part, and there was a lot of giggling when the four of them saw what they would be wearing. By now they were all slightly silly with excitement.

The ancient clothes were faded and frayed and smelt of dusty museums. Lily and Silver were given long dresses of thick, dark green woolly material, with huge skirts and stiff tops like corsets. Their hair was bundled away into tight white caps. Oz and Caydon had baggy, knee-length breeches, short jackets and big black hats. They all had to wear withered antique shoes with wooden soles.

"I'm glad nobody from school can see us," Oz said. "We look like a bunch of scarecrows."

"Look on the bright side," Caydon said cheerfully, studying himself in the mirror the professor held up. "At least we'll blend in. And it's a lot better than suddenly finding ourselves stark-naked in the middle of history."

Once they were all kitted out in their mouldy costumes, Silver took them to an SMU shooting gallery in the basement of the MI6 building, where a grey-haired army sergeant issued them with seventeenth-century muskets and showed them how to make antique bullets with little lead balls and gunpowder.

"This takes ages!" Oz complained. "By the time I've loaded the gun, I'll be dead! James Bond wouldn't get far with one of these."

"Why can't we have real guns?" Caydon wanted to know.

The sergeant said modern guns could not be transported back in time, and made them do an hour of target practice. Oz had the best aim, Caydon was the fastest loader – and Lily was so useless that she nearly shot the sergeant.

"I'm rubbish – I'll never be able to do this!"

"Don't worry," Silver said, "I'll take care of you – I've used one of these before."

Lily did better with the funny little metal device they were given after the shooting lesson.

"This is a tinderbox," J explained. "Matches weren't invented in the seventeenth century. A tinderbox makes a spark by striking steel against flint. The spark lights the dry cotton wick, and that makes a flame to start a fire."

The metal box had a small handle at the side; you pressed it to strike the flint and steel together. Oz couldn't get a single spark for ages. Caydon managed one spark, which set fire to his breeches. Lily managed to light a pile of dry straw at her first go.

"Excellent," J said. "I'll put you in charge of the tinderbox and the boys can have the muskets. And you'll all be carrying swords, naturally."

"Swords!" Lily squeaked.

The antique swords came from the Museum of London. The children buckled the leather belts around their waists, and Oz and Caydon practised whisking the blades out of their scabbards like people in a film, until J said, "Don't use any weapon unless your lives are in danger. Remember that anything you do in the past could have a knock-on effect in the present – look what happened when Demerara spent just a few minutes in the Elizabethan age."

"I suppose if we killed someone," Caydon said, "lots of people wouldn't get born."

"Precisely. Stay out of sight as much as possible and try not to speak to anyone." He turned solemnly to Silver. "I don't need to tell you this will be the hardest job you've ever done for the department. Good luck."

"Thank you, sir." The seventeenth-century Silver, in her long green dress, stood to attention.

"Good luck, all of you. Remember, your mission is to spoil D33's plan – and make sure London burns. What you're doing might seem horrible and cruel, but you mustn't allow yourselves to weaken."

Oz said what they'd all been thinking. "But we'll be killing people."

"There were six recorded deaths in the Great Fire," J said. "More deaths went unrecorded, of course – but the numbers were tiny, compared with the thousands who will die if Alba gets her way. Remember that."

A car with darkened windows took the four children through the quiet Sunday city, eastwards along the Thames. They got out beside a tall stone column, with gold flames carved at the top. It was at least as tall as Nelson's Column in Trafalgar Square.

"It's called The Monument," Silver said. "It was designed by Sir Christopher Wren as a memorial of the Great Fire. You can go inside and climb up to the top – I did it in 1888, when I visited with my parents. There are three hundred and eleven steps."

Oz said, "If we don't start the fire, this thing won't exist when we come back."

The streets around the monument were cordoned off with plastic police tape, and there were groups of armed police on every corner.

One of the policemen came to meet them. "Hi, kids – Rosie said I'd run into you."

It was their old friend Alan, from the SMU branch of the river police. They had met him during their last adventure, and he was engaged to Rosie from the commando unit. He was a tall, strongly built young man, with very blond hair and pink skin.

Lily hugged him, and he did high fives with Oz and Caydon.

"And this is Silver, our vampire bodyguard," Lily said.

"Hi, Silver," Alan said. "Wow, look at you all – you're like something in an old painting!"

"Don't rub it in, mate," Caydon said. "We feel stupid enough."

Alan chuckled. "Sorry. As you can see we're right beside the river, so the river police are in charge of this operation – and it's a good thing this is a Sunday and none of the office workers are here to get in the way. My orders are to take you to the exact site of Pudding Lane, where the Great Fire started. Keep close together, now."

The buildings here were all brand-new offices, with walls of shining glass. It was very odd to see their tattered seventeenth-century reflections as Alan led them down the deserted narrow streets.

They stopped at a very ordinary modern printing shop. "This is the nearest we could get," Alan said. "It should bring you within five metres."

Demerara and Spike were waiting on the desk beside the till. Demerara had a piece of see-through plaster stuck across her mouth and her bright green eyes were boiling with fury.

Lily went to stroke her. "What happened to her mouth?"

"J's orders," Spike piped up. "The old girl just can't seem to remember that she's forbidden to talk – and a talking cat will get the lot of you burned as witches back in the seventeenth century. So J taped her mouth up to be absolutely sure."

Demerara quivered. "Mmmmmgh!" she shouted through the strip of plaster.

"Never mind." Lily tried not to smile at how funny the cat looked. "It won't be for long."

"I'm afraid I can't take it off," Silver told her. "But I'll give you an extra conditioning treatment when we get back, and put some lovely pink glitter in your fur."

Silver adored Demerara, and (unlike Lily) never got tired of being her beautician.

"Mmmmgh!" Demerara sounded a little less angry, and allowed Lily to pick her up.

Alan saluted Silver. "Over to you, Major."

"Wow," Lily said. "You're a major?"

Caydon gave a snort of laughter. "No wonder she's so bossy!"

Lily was about to snap that Silver was only bossy because she was protecting them – but the serious look on Silver's face stopped her. They didn't need an argument now.

"Stand in a circle, please," Silver said quietly. "Spike, get inside Oz's hat. And Demerara, you can ride on Lily's shoulders."

Oz scooped up the rat and stowed him inside his hat – his little feet felt very sharp on his scalp. Demerara draped herself around Lily's shoulders, like a stout, heavy, furry scarf.

Silver took a small piece of paper from the sleeve of her dress. She unwrapped it carefully; it contained six tiny balls of chocolate. "These are made of the chocolate from the leg of the phoenix. If the time scientist has got his sums right, they'll keep us in the past for at least three hours. Put one on your tongue and join hands."

"But what about Demerara?" Lily asked. "Shall I take the tape off her mouth?"

"I'll do it." Silver came over and gently peeled away the plaster.

"It's a disgrace and an OUTRAGE! I will NOT have a dirty great piece of plast— Mmmmmmgh!"

Silver had neatly slipped in the chocolate and sealed her up again.

"Cor, it's funny when the old girl can't talk!" Spike poked his head out under the hat to swallow his piece of chocolate. "It's the first time she's shut up since the bank holiday in 1973 when she tried to eat a toffee!"

Lily put the little ball of chocolate on her tongue. There was a slight warmth as it melted against the top of her mouth. She grasped the hand of Oz on one side and Silver on the other, and an electric charge of power shot around the circle.

Lily had imagined that going back in time would be like flying. It was more like the earthquake machine she'd stood on once at the science museum – the ground kept shifting and changing, rising and falling under their feet, and it took all her concentration not to fall over. There was a great rushing, whooshing sound, of crashing waves and tearing wind.

And then it was suddenly quiet. They were standing on a narrow, dark street, in the middle of a muddy puddle. For a moment they clutched one another's hands in breathless silence.

"OK," Silver whispered. "We're here."

13

The Prisoner of Pudding Lane

Oz took a deep breath of seventeenth-century air. "Yuck that smell!"

The darkness smelt of dirty river water and woodsmoke, and something disgusting that made them all pull faces.

"Oh, no!" Lily whispered. "It's the stench of evil again!"

"Actually, it's just the stench of normal poo," said Silver. "There's a lot of poo about in the past. Try to ignore it."

None of them – except Silver – had ever seen a street without street lights. The darkness was scarily deep, but after a few minutes their eyes began to adjust. One feeble light shone in an upstairs window.

"I think this is the baker's shop." Silver screwed up her eyes to read the wooden sign. THOMAS FARRINER, BAKER TO THE KING.

Somewhere in the darkness above them, a bell began to toll. More bells tolled across the city. Somewhere behind the crooked row of wooden-framed houses, a man's voice called, "Twelve of the clock and all's well!"

"Great, we're bang on time," Silver said. She nudged the rat sitting at her feet with her shoe. "Spike, go and look through the window, see if it's clear."

"That's not me, boss," Spike squeaked from Oz's shoulder. "He's one of the locals."

"Yuck!" Lily shrank back against the wall. "It ran over my foot!"

"Rats live more out in the open in this century," Spike said. "There's about twenty of them milling about on this street right now, bold as brass."

"Yuck! Oh, I'm sorry, Spike. I know you're a rat and I love you – but I can't stand normal rats!"

"MMMMGH!" Demerara roared inside her plaster. Her golden paws swiped angrily at her sealed mouth.

"Keep hold of her, Lily," said Silver. "Demerara, keep still and that's an order!"

Lily began to see what a good thing it was that Demerara's motor mouth had been taped up. The cat was wriggling furiously and obviously trying to let forth a stream of abuse.

"Give me a sec and I'll see if I can get any info." Spike ran down Oz's arm and jumped into the muddy, smelly puddle at their feet. "Rats always know what's going on."

It was fascinating to see the way the seventeenth-century rats gathered around Spike. There was a chorus of jagged squeaks — Caydon thought they sounded electronic — and after about five minutes Spike ran breathlessly back to Oz.

"Yes, it's really me — pick me up."

Oz bent down to scoop him up. He didn't mind rats as much as Lily did, but he didn't like them and the thought of touching an antique rat was creepy. He remembered that it was the rats who had brought the plague, because they were covered with infected fleas — yuck! He was glad to know that the one on his arm was good old Spike.

"Well?" Silver asked.

"Well, boss, at first all they wanted to talk about was who had what food. But then one of them asked if I'd come to rescue the prisoner."

"Prisoner?" Silver looked blank. "There's nothing about a prisoner in my orders."

"They say he's an old man with a white beard," Spike went on. "He's chained up where that light is."

"If he's in chains he won't be able to escape from the fire," Oz said. "We should set him free."

"We'll have time after we've got the fire going," Caydon said. "It won't take long – it's the house next door to the baker's."

"But the big news," Spike said, "is that Master and Mistress Farriner are tied up and gagged in the back of the shop – looks like D33 got here first."

"Great, it's all going according to plan," Silver whispered. "Spike, run inside the house and see what's happening."

"OK, boss!" The talking rat leapt off Oz's arm, into the darkness.

Oz looked at the sleeve where Spike had been. "Hey, my clothes have turned new!"

"I thought my shoes felt more comfortable," Caydon said. "And the holes in my jacket have gone."

Silver hissed, "Quiet!"

The rats suddenly scattered and vanished. At the other end of Pudding Lane they heard some men laughing and a woman calling out "Goodnight!"

"I feel a bit guilty," Lily whispered. "If our mission's a success, they won't have any houses tomorrow. I wish we could warn them."

After what seemed like ages but was really only a few minutes, Spike came back.

"It's true, the baker and his wife are tied up – and there's a witch in there. Rats can always spot a witch."

"Right, follow me." Silver crept along the wall, feeling

her way to the door of the baker's shop. "These houses are all made of wood – I'm not surprised London burned down," she whispered.

The door of the shop was open. Putting her finger to her lips, Silver beckoned them all inside. The dark shop had a comforting smell of flour and fresh bread. A door at the back of the shop was slightly open. They saw light around the crack, and heard a woman's voice:

"I'm not robbing you – I don't want any of this antique crap! But you're staying there until I've put out your fire to the last cinder – you were very careless, you know. You nearly burned down the whole city!"

There was a sound of splashing, as if the woman was throwing water, a great hissing sound and a smell of wet bonfire.

"OK, I expect someone will come along to untie you in the morning." This witch had a very modern-sounding voice. "And thanks for the dress, Mistress Farriner – I just wish you weren't so fat!"

Dim light crept into the shop as she opened the door. The children and animals shrank into the tangle of shadows around the walls, hardly daring to breathe.

The witch was tall and slim and surprisingly good-looking, wearing a seventeenth-century dress that was several sizes too big. She halted for a second and sniffed thoughtfully, as if she smelt something curious. Lily felt Silver twitch with alarm beside her.

The witch shrugged to herself and took a large key from the baggy bosom of her dress. She stepped out of the shop and hurried next door. A moment later they heard her unlocking the front door.

"The prisoner!" Spike snuffled into Silver's ear.

"You lot stay out of sight," muttered Silver. "I want to see what she's up to." She crept a few steps forward, her hand on her sword.

"I do wish SOMEONE would tell me what's going on," a man's voice grumbled, out in the street. "Where on earth am I? Why am I wearing chains? And these ridiculous clothes? And what have you done with Greta?"

"That's Dr Spatz!" gasped Oz.

"For pity's sake, Ludo!" snapped the witch. "Stop whining!"

Dr Spatz's voice said, "I think I have a right to know where you're taking me."

"To Alba, that's where – and bad luck for you if her spell hasn't worked!"

"But I've told you everything I know. Twelvey, I insist that you take me back to Gospel Oak!"

"Twelvey!" Lily grabbed Silver's skirt. "It's Greta's mother!"

There was silence for a moment then. "Whoops," said Twelvey. "I've left the light on."

She snapped her fingers and the dim light in the back room went out, engulfing the children in darkness.

Oz hissed, "We've got to find out where she's taking Dr Spatz!"

Silver's voice was anxious. "But it's not in my orders."

"Never mind your orders — we can't just leave him in the past. Let me follow them!"

"No!" Silver whispered. She was trying to think quickly. "I can't let you loose on the streets of seventeenth-century London – it's far too dangerous. Spike and Demerara, you follow Dr Spatz and Twelvey, and then run back here to tell us where they are. Demerara, I'll take off your plaster if you PROMISE to keep your mouth SHUT!"

Even the fussy little cat could see that this was a serious situation, and she nodded her golden head. Silver peeled off the plaster and Demerara and Spike vanished into the shadows after Dr Spatz and his witch-wife. Lily made an effort not to think the terrible thought that she might never see her cat again.

"It's safer for the animals," Silver said. "They're better at navigating in the dark, and they know how to stay out of sight. Now, come on – Lily, have the tinderbox ready."

"I can't see a thing — oh!" Lily felt Silver's hand reaching into the bag tied around her waist, in which she was carrying the tinderbox.

"Vampires don't have a problem with seeing in the dark," Silver said. "I'll take the tinderbox and find a candle."

A moment later they were blinking in the very dim

light of a single candle. Silver led them into the room behind the shop, where the baker and his wife were sitting, bound, gagged and lashed to chairs, big-eyed with terror.

"Oh, the poor things!" Lily cried out.

"Leave them," Silver said. "We can only set them free once the fire has started. We can't have them raising the alarm and putting it out. If Twelvey hadn't interfered, they'd be asleep in bed."

They all looked round the small back room. There was a large baker's oven – but everything was soaking wet and the stone floor was awash with sooty black water.

"We'll never get a fire started in here," Oz said. "Not with one candle and one tinderbox."

"I'll get some dry wood— Drat!" Silver opened the box of logs for the fire. "This is wet too!"

The whole room, including the baker and his wife, was dripping with water. Twelvey had done her job thoroughly.

"We're the only dry things here," Silver said. "I've got it – Lily and I can burn our petticoats!"

They were both wearing calico petticoats under their big skirts. They quickly wriggled out of them (luckily they could do this without removing their dresses), taking care not to drag them on the wet floor. The boys helped them to tear the petticoats into thin strips.

"I never thought it would be this difficult to start a

fire," Caydon said. "In films people just light one match and up it goes."

Silver lit all the candles she could find – there were five in the room – and piled the cotton rags around the candle flames. The rags smouldered but refused to catch fire.

"Blow harder!" Silver shouted.

They all blew frantically on the piles of smoking rags, until the sparks caught and turned to fragile flames. Silver placed the rags around the front of the shop and up the wooden staircase. The smell of burning became sharper and stronger, and the smoke made their eyes sting.

The baker and his wife coughed and squealed behind their gags. The floor was full of moving black shadows, streaking past their ankles.

"The rats are leaving," Silver said. "That means the fire's taken hold. We'd better carry Mr and Mrs Farriner out."

The baker was a small man, and Oz and Caydon carried his chair out into the street fairly easily. Silver, with her superhuman vampire strength, hefted his stout wife from the house. The bewildered couple wriggled and coughed and tried to shout for help, but Silver said, "Sorry about this," and touched their necks with the palm of her hand until they flopped into unconsciousness.

"Did you – kill them?" Lily asked fearfully.

"No," Silver said. "I did my vampire stun grip – it's a

trick we used before the treatment, to stun people before we bit them."

"That's just like the Vulcan death grip in *Star Trek*," Caydon said. "I wish I could do that – I'd stun Ms Shah before maths lessons."

Silver dragged the baker and his wife down a narrow alley and turned back to stare at the shop. A long black line of rats was filing out of the front door – many holding chunks of bread in their mouths. A tongue of orange flame licked at the thatched roof of the baker's shop. Smoke and sparks poured from the thatch of the house next door.

"I think we've done it," Silver said quietly. "The Great Fire of London has officially started."

14

Sons of Alba

The people of Pudding Lane had begun to take notice of the fire. They were running out of the narrow, higgledy-piggledy houses in their long nightgowns, yelling and bumping into each other. A woman with a baby tried to count her excited children. Two men on the roof of the baker's shop were pouring buckets of water on the blazing thatch. Two more men were swinging axes at the house next door, trying to pull it down before the fire could spread.

Lily cowered in the mouth of the alley, trying to keep out of sight. Something tugged at her skirt. She looked down to see the eyes of Spike and Demerara gleaming in the shadows.

"We followed them!" mewed Demerara. "They went into a big castle!"

"It's the one that gets burned down in the Great Fire," Spike said breathlessly. "There are soldiers at the gate, but we found a little window you should be able to squeeze through."

"And I didn't say a single word, did I, Spike? So you don't need to tape my mouth again."

Oz, Lily and Caydon looked at one another. Their official work was done, but they all hated the thought of leaving Dr Spatz behind in the past to be barbecued.

"It'll be dangerous," Silver said. "None of us has clearance for direct dealings with D33."

"But we can't just go without him," Oz said. "Not now we've seen him. We've got time to rescue him before the chocolate wears off, haven't we?"

"Yes, but we've also got time to get killed," Lily said, with a shiver. "And then we'd go back to the future as dead bodies."

"Don't be such a wimp." Caydon was scornful. "If we listened to you we'd never do anything!"

Lily turned to him angrily. "And if we listened to your silly ideas—"

"Shut up, both of you!" snapped Silver. "I'm trying to think."

"I do wish you two wouldn't argue all the time," Demerara said. "It's so unhelpful."

Caydon gave a sudden snort of laughter. "Look who's talking! You never stop fighting with Spike!"

"Nonsense!" The cat was offended. "I'm merely giving an ignorant rat the benefit of my superior WISDOM!"

"That's right," Spike chuckled. "She's got the temper of a blooming angel!"

The rat's dirty, furry face, with its bright little eyes, looked so funny and so kind that they all relaxed into smiles, and Lily felt braver. She took Silver's hand. "Look, I'm really scared and I want to go home – but poor Greta will be so sad if anything happens to Dr Spatz. She doesn't have anybody else, except her mean mother. We ought to try, at least."

"And we're armed," Caydon added. He was longing for a chance to use his sword.

"Well – OK," Silver said. "But you've all got to follow my orders exactly. Unlike me and the animals, you three are mortal – and if I bring you back dead, that's my promotion down the pan." She tried to smile, but her face in the dim orange glow of the flames was deathly pale. "Seriously, do as you're told. Keep close together."

Spike curled on Silver's shoulder to squeak directions into her ear, and they set off towards the castle. It was like being in a foreign city. At first they were walking against a tide of people running to see the fire in Pudding Lane. But they lost the fire surprisingly quickly, as they hurried through a dark maze of narrow, crooked streets. The river, when they suddenly came upon it, was shocking because there was no embankment and the familiar Thames had been replaced with an endless muddy beach. They passed noisy taverns, where men fought and women screamed, and Spike had to bite the hand of a man who made a sudden grab for Silver. They tripped over sleeping beggars and sloshed through heaps of stinking mud.

Baynard's Castle loomed at them in the darkness. It was easier to see now, and when he turned round Oz understood why the sky over Pudding Lane was glowing red; the fire they had started was lighting the city like a dull orange lamp.

It was very odd to see this strange building, knowing that it was the last day of its existence. In a couple of days, if the Great Fire went to plan, the imposing castle would be a heap of charred rubble.

Caydon asked, "What's up with the Thames?"

Beside the red-brick towers of the castle, the river had grown another muddy, meandering branch.

"That's not the Thames," Silver said. "That's the Fleet River – it used to run down to the Thames from Hampstead, until the Victorians turned it into a sewer."

Lily buried her nose in her sleeve. "It smells like it's a sewer already!"

"But what did they do with it? Where did they put it?"

"They covered it up," Silver said. "The Fleet's still there in our time, but it's underground."

"Boss!" Spike hissed into Silver's ear. "See where that light is? That's the sentry post at the back gate and it's got four soldiers in it."

"They're not very nice," Demerara said. "One of them stabbed Spike with his sword – right through, just like a kebab."

"Yes, and he didn't half get a shock when I wriggled off the blade and ran away!" Spike let out a high squeal of laughter. "He was drunk as a skunk and thought he was seeing things!"

The light in the sky was getting brighter. Shouts and the sound of running feet could be heard all through the crooked streets. The air was hot and sour in their nostrils.

A soldier, wearing a huge metal helmet like a coal-bucket and a metal breastplate, came out of the wooden hut inside the castle gate to look at the sky. "Another fire, over in the city," they heard him call cheerfully over his shoulder. "'Tis well we have the river to protect us!" He went back inside, yawning noisily.

Silver put her finger on her lips. Sticking to the darkest places, she led them to the castle's back gate. They dashed through the gate past the sentry post, and into a dull inner courtyard surrounded by dark windows.

"This place is huge!" Oz whispered. "How will we find Dr Spatz?"

"We've got it all worked out," Demerara said proudly. "Haven't we, Spike?" She pointed with her front paw to a window set very low in one wall. "You lot wait for us there."

"Shan't be long," added Spike. "Keep your peckers up!" Once more, the rat and the cat vanished silently into the darkness.

"This is crazy," muttered Silver. "I don't know what I'm going to tell my mum."

They crept towards the low window, which was hidden from the guards by the bulk of a big stone buttress.

"Their security's rubbish," Oz said. "This is nothing like MI6."

Spike and Demerara seemed to be away for ages, and Lily began to worry that they had been captured, but Silver pointed out that waiting always made time feel twice as long. While they waited, they listened to the yells of "FIRE!" over towards Pudding Lane.

"I think it's getting closer," Caydon said. "It's funny, I keep expecting to hear sirens, but they won't be invented for hundreds of years. Is there even a fire brigade yet?"

"No, the official Fire Service is quite a new thing," Silver said. "In the seventeenth century all anybody can do is pour water on the thatched roofs and pull houses down so the fire doesn't spread. But it doesn't always work. When we were living in Transylvania in the 1860s, the villagers set fire to our castle and we just had to flee." Silver sounded younger when she talked about her lonely vampire past. "We did a lot of fleeing before the treatment."

"Well, I think history totally SUCKS," Caydon

announced. "And I'm going to say so next time we have a history lesson. It's dark and cold and it stinks of poo."

"And I don't want to think what I might be sitting on," Oz said.

"Psst!" someone hissed, on the other side of the low window.

Silver bent her head down. "Spike?"

"We've pulled the bolt," Spike said. "Now you can just push it open and climb in – but keep quiet!"

Silver pushed at the muddy window. It was made of heavy metal with no glass in it. She held it open while the twins and Caydon climbed through. The opening was small and Lily and Silver had a struggle with their big skirts – the material was stiffer and harder to handle now that it was new again.

One by one they dropped down from the window into a large basement room with a vaulted stone ceiling. "This is the castle kitchen," Demerara whispered. "Unfortunately they don't leave any food lying about." The only light came from the glowing embers of the enormous fire in the great, yawning fireplace. Three young men were asleep on the floor in front of it. Three fat tabby cats slept beside them. And beside the biggest of the cats lay the stiff body of a dead rat.

"Spike, get out of sight," Silver whispered. "We don't have time for that brute to wake up and chase you."

Spike hid himself inside Oz's hat. As quietly as they

could, they tiptoed past the sleeping cooks and cats. Lily suddenly remembered a picture of Sleeping Beauty's castle in a book she'd liked when she was little, showing the cooks in the kitchen fast asleep with the ladles still in their hands.

Beyond the kitchen door was a dank, empty corridor and a spiralling stone staircase. "Up to the next floor," squeaked Spike.

In modern buildings there is always light. It was very confusing to walk through the doomed castle where the only scraps of light came from open doors or a servant carrying a candle in a distant passageway.

The immortal animals, however, were not navigating with their eyes. Demerara halted suddenly and sniffed. "This smells familiar."

"Yes, I'm picking up a whiff of witches," Spike said. "Take your hat off, Oz, and let me out." He jumped off Oz's head on to Demerara's back. "See that little door? Push it open then get down on your hands and knees. We'll be fine as long as we keep out of sight. The witches won't smell us because none of us smells mortal – not even you kids, thanks to those genes of yours."

Silver opened a door of carved wood and they dropped on to all fours. Oz saw why they had to crawl when suddenly they came out in a small gallery, high up in the wall of a huge room. He peered down through the gap in the wooden railing and his heart flipped with shock.

Dr Spatz stood in the middle of the floor. He was wearing a long brown robe; his arms were chained tightly to his body. Two women sat at a big polished table. One was Twelvey, trying not to fall out of the baker's wife's enormous dress. The other one was dressed in a grand gown of black velvet, covered with rich gold embroidery. She lifted her head to glare at Dr Spatz – and Oz heard Caydon drawing in a breath of horror.

They were looking down at Alba, eldest daughter of the Emperor Diocletian and head of D33. She was tall and dark and rather handsome-looking – but it was a bad face, with eyes that were both nasty and horribly, sickeningly sad. The light from dozens of candles covered the walls in a ghostly, flickering web of shadows.

"I just don't understand," Alba said. "I should've been able to free my boys! But I couldn't open the door – it wouldn't budge, even for me. I could only shout to them through a grating. If I can't reach my boys we can't work on our relationship – and I won't be able to unleash the forces of darkness. I tell you, something has gone wrong!"

"Did the boys know who you were?" asked Twelvey.

"Eventually," Alba snarled. "I'd forgotten how thick they are – just like their father."

"Who was their father again?"

"Oh, Twelvey, do keep up! He was the giant I had that thing with when we first came here."

"Oh, yes. You always liked your husbands big and stupid."

"I tried to talk to my boys about rebuilding our relationship — but they weren't interested! They kept grunting about some pet I gave them that got confiscated by the government. It was very disappointing. And my plan is so simple! If I can free my twins, I'll have the power to run riot all over this city!"

"I thought it was all about parenting," Twelvey said.

"Of course that's part of it. But it just so happens that I can do a lot more if my boys are onside, and I can't imagine why they won't cooperate. I don't have control of the nation — and I don't know what I'm going to tell my parenting guru... You must've done something WRONG!"

Twelvey scowled. "I did NOT — ask Ludo!"

"It's quite true," Dr Spatz said. "She put out every scrap of fire."

"You shut up," Alba snapped at him. "I don't know why Twelvey didn't kill you years ago. It's your fault she never bonded properly with that useless daughter of hers. How could she teach the girl to be properly wicked with you bumbling about?" She stopped, and sniffed at the air. "Are you wearing a new perfume?"

"No," Twelvey said. She sniffed too. "There's a smell like evening primrose. Funnily enough, I thought I caught a whiff of it in the baker's shop. It reminded me of something, but I couldn't think what."

High up in the gallery, everyone was still and silent, and thinking the same thing: she can smell us.

"Hmm," Alba said thoughtfully. "Me too – I expect it'll come back to me."

"Excuse me, Alba," Dr Spatz said. "I know you've never liked me – but now you've got the chocolate phoenix and I've told you everything I know about the carriers, please send me home to my own time!"

"Certainly not – you know far too much about my plans and you'll blab to the SMU. Don't make a mess when you kill him, Twelvey – I suggest you wait for high tide and then chuck him in the river."

A heavy door crashed open suddenly, shaking the room. A nun in a black dress and black veil ran in – a nun with the unmistakably evil face of one of the thirty-three wicked sisters.

"Secunda," Alba said, "what are you doing here? I told you to kidnap King Charles."

Secunda was agitated and out of breath. "Too late – it's all gone wrong – the fire's started!"

"WHAT?"

"The wind's blowing the flames into a huge ball of fire!"

"I told you to stop the wind!" Alba roared.

"Well, I couldn't – OK? The Great Fire has started, and that means the time stitch has been tampered with!"

"Don't look at me," Twelvey said crossly.

Alba leapt to her feet. "That smell – I've remembered it!" She brought her fist down on the table so hard that a great crack appeared. "THAT'S HOW NONA'S FARTS SMELLED AFTER SHE MET THAT BLOODY SAINT!"

"Good grief, that's it!" cried Twelvey. "That lovely smell was how we found out Nona and Undy had turned good!"

"CARRIERS!" screamed Alba. The sound was agonizing. "I SMELL CARRIERS!"

"Run," muttered Silver. "Run for your lives!"

But running meant crawling – back along the gallery, which took longer than it should have because they kept getting tangled in the huge skirts of Lily and Silver's dresses. Lily was shaking so much that Oz and Silver had to drag her out by her arms.

"This way!" Silver pushed them back along the corridor.

"Stop right there!"

Twelvey stood in front of them, her eyes glittering wickedly in the light of her candle.

They froze.

This is it, we've been caught, and now we're finished, Lily and Oz told each other inside their heads.

The witch slowly lifted her arm.

Instead of casting some terrible spell, however, Twelvey dragged Dr Spatz out of the shadows and shoved him at them roughly.

"Take him – do you hear me? Take the old fool back to his own time."

"Twelvey, darling — I thought you were going to kill me!" cried Dr Spatz.

"Of course I'm not going to kill you! But Alba must never find out, do you hear? You'll pass through all right if you travel with the carriers."

"Hang on," Silver said, "we don't know when we're going back; it depends when the chocolate wears off."

"I'll send you through our portal," Twelvey said. "It's always much easier to return to your own time than it is to travel to a new one."

"Where's the portal?"

"Right here!" The witch pushed them all towards a wooden door beside the staircase. When she opened it they all moaned at the stink. "This is a working magic portal and you can make your escape through here. It's the castle garderobe."

Lily asked, "What's a garderobe?"

"The old name for a toilet," Silver said, wrinkling her nose. It was a draughty hole that went right down to the smelly river far below.

"Great," Caydon said. "We're escaping down a toilet."

Oz and Lily giggled at this, in the way that you giggle when you're trembling with nerves.

"I don't get it," Silver said. "Why're you helping Dr Spatz when it was you who kidnapped him in the first place?"

Twelvey scowled. "He's the father of my daughter, and

when you have a child with a human, something rubs off – call it love, if you insist."

"Oh, darling," sighed Dr Spatz. "We had some great times, didn't we?"

"You old nincompoop!" His wife stamped her foot impatiently. "Get down that crapper before my sisters find you!"

"But I won't fit in there – HEY!"

Twelvey picked up Dr Spatz by the neck of his robe and bundled him head first down the seventeenth-century toilet. He was a tight fit. She jumped hard on his bottom to push him through.

Oz, Lily and Caydon were not giggling now. They watched with their hearts in their mouths.

"AARRGH!" screamed Dr Spatz. "T – W – E – L—"

There was a sudden eerie silence, as if someone had switched off a radio.

"I hope he's gone to the right year," Silver said. "Come on, let's get moving – Spike and Demerara, you jump in next."

"In there? My dear Silver, Spike is a rat and he's used to poo – he even likes it – but I am a refined—"

"Quickly – before I put the plaster back on your mouth—"

"Oh, all right!" Demerara screwed up her golden face and jumped huffily through the hole.

Spike leapt after her with a cry of "WHEEE!"

"I'll go next," Caydon said. "Get it over with." He grinned and dived in head first.

Lily turned to Twelvey. "Thank you for saving us."

The witch tried to scowl again, but this time there was more sadness in her face than anger. "No soppiness," she muttered. "Say hi to Greta for me."

Diving into an antique toilet was an experience Lily wanted to forget as quickly as possible. She stuck her head into the hole, gagging at the smell. For a moment she was stuck, hanging upside down in a slimy brick tunnel.

The darkness changed to emptiness, the terrible smell evaporated and the wind around her became a hurricane. She was whirling like a leaf in a storm, too shaken to be scared.

And then there was light – proper, bright, electric light – and she was lying on a smooth, dry floor. She sat up. She was still wearing her seventeenth-century dress but the material had turned ancient again. "Are we back?" she asked.

Silver untangled herself from Caydon and Oz. "Oh, how lovely!" Her eyes shone with happiness and relief. "She's sent us to the north London portal – and it's in the basement of our house!"

15

Incident in Muswell Hill

Lily's heart was as light as a feather, and she could see that the others felt the same. They had returned from the scary depths of the past to Silver's friendly house in Plum Terrace, and they were safe – for the moment, at least.

Silver's mother burst into the small, white-painted cellar, amazed and delighted to see them. "Darling – we didn't expect you to turn up here! How on earth did you manage to work the portal? Oh, never mind, you're safe, and that's all that matters!" She hugged the children and animals, and fetched her husband's bathrobe for Dr Spatz, who was hiding behind a table because he was stark-naked.

"Thank you. Most embarrassing – I felt my clothes disintegrating somewhere around the 1780s."

Once he was decently covered they all moved up to the neat but eccentric kitchen. Cathy made tea, minced some raw chicken for Demerara and went back to the cellar to make her report. Vaz put down his orange knitting and gave everyone slices of home-made carrot cake.

"This is great, Dad," Silver said. "Phew – it's such a relief to be back!"

"It's wonderful," Caydon said. "I love modern times."

Oz said, "I can't stop looking at the electric lights." He yawned until his eyes watered. "I don't think I've ever been so tired in my life. This has been the longest day in history."

"You came back early," Vaz said. "It's only teatime."

Lily caught the yawn. "I hope J doesn't need us for anything else. I want to go home."

"Yes," Dr Spatz said, "could you call me a minicab?"

Vaz shook his head. "Sorry, man. You've got a few questions to answer."

"Where's Greta? Is she all right?"

"Chillax – Greta's fine."

"Thank goodness!" Dr Spatz sighed with his mouth full. "Oh, this cake is beautiful! You can't imagine the food I've been eating in the past!"

Cathy came back into the room. "J told me to say well done, and you'll be glad to hear that you haven't come back to the cruel reign of King Brian. Thanks to you lot, the Great Fire of London went ahead as planned, and Alba was foiled."

They all smiled at this.

"Do you want the full report now, Mum?" Silver asked. "I'm afraid we left the muskets behind in Pudding Lane."

"The report can wait." Cathy stroked Silver's hair. "You've done more than enough for one day. Dr Spatz has to go into custody, but you can relax now, darling – and you three can go home."

Demerara daintily wiped her mouth with her paw. "Silver will have to come with us. She promised she'd give me glittery fur – and that kitchen window in the past RUINED my claw polish."

Lily and Silver looked at each other and burst out laughing. "Typical Demerara," said Lily. "We nearly die saving history from magical terrorists, but all she cares about is her claw polish!" A brilliant idea came to her. "Silver, why don't you come back with us and stay the night? We've got a blow-up mattress; we could put it on the floor next to my bed."

"Well," Cathy said doubtfully, "it is a school night—"

"A sleepover!" Silver's face was alight with longing. "Please, Mum! You know I've always wanted to have a real sleepover. We're never in a place long enough to make friends – and vampires never get invited anywhere. Please!"

"Oh, go on then." Cathy kissed her daughter's cheek. "If Lily's parents don't mind."

Silver let out a shriek of joy and it was settled. A

government car dropped off their modern clothes, and they all removed their seventeenth-century costumes and walked round the corner to Skittle Street.

"I love my trainers," Oz said. "It's like walking on air after those stupid antique clogs."

Caydon took a big, noisy breath. "Doesn't modern London smell fantastic?"

"I liked the seventeenth century," Spike chuckled, from Caydon's shoulder. "It looked great for rats — I might retire there."

Skittle Street was still crowded with ghostly soldiers, who stood to attention and saluted as Silver passed them. She was so excited about her first sleepover that she forgot to salute back.

"Seriously — your mum won't mind, will she?"

"I don't think so," Lily said. "She'll be so pleased that I'm finally having a friend to stay. This is my first sleepover too."

"Really?"

"Yes, and I don't have the excuse of being a vampire. At my last school the other girls thought I was weird, and at this school you're the only person who knows I live with talking animals."

Just as she had predicted, Lily's mum was delighted that she was having a friend to stay over, even though it was a school night. Caydon went home to Elvira and his mother, Oz went to his room to catch up on his violin practice, and Silver and Lily had a very nice and totally normal Sunday afternoon and evening. They combed glittery body gel into Demerara's golden fur and painted her claws pink, and Silver was radiant.

Best of all, Mum let the two girls play with baby Daisy while she sploshed about in her little plastic bath.

"She's just SO scrumptious!" Silver sighed, when she was lying on the blow-up mattress beside Lily's bed. "All fluffy and warm and pink – you are SO lucky! My parents were going to try to have another baby, because they knew how much I wanted a little brother or sister. But then they were turned into vampires."

"Can't vampires have babies?"

"No – not even with IVF."

The lamp had been switched off, and the only light came from Lily's two strings of coloured fairy lights. Demerara was fast asleep at the end of the bed. The girls were whispering; it was late and they were supposed to be asleep too.

"I hardly ever get the chance to see a baby," Silver said. "When we lived in Transylvania, one of our vampire neighbours had the sweetest baby boy and I loved playing with him. But it made my mum unhappy."

"Why?"

"Because she knew he'd always be a baby and never grow up. It makes her sad that I'll always be eleven."

"*Look, the vampire's here again,*" a tiny, sharp voice

said, somewhere on the wall. *"I'm getting used to the smell."*

"Me too," another tiny voice squeaked. *"And she's quite nice when you get to know her."*

"This is another reason I never have sleepovers," Lily said. "How would I explain my talking wallpaper?"

Silver said, "I'm glad your roses like me now. Thanks for giving me such a fantastic time this evening."

Lily yawned. "Sorry it was so ordinary. But that's what I needed after all the time travel."

"Yes," Silver said wistfully. "Sometimes being ordinary is the most wonderful thing in the world."

"It's Halloween this Saturday," Caydon said. "And I've never been less interested."

"I used to think Halloween was a laugh," Oz agreed, with his mouth full of cereal bar. "But it seems pointless dressing up as witches and vampires when you've seen the real thing."

"We ARE the real thing," Silver said, and they all giggled.

It was morning break and the four of them were in the playground at Sir Richard Whittington, a bare and windy space with a few knobbly, defiant trees. They had managed to get the concrete bench beside the bike shelter.

"I'm a bit disappointed we've got school today," Lily

said. "I thought we'd be summoned to give our reports. I was hoping we'd go back to the seaside."

Silver said, "They need to analyse the time fabric first, to make sure nothing's been damaged. And they're still interrogating poor old Dr Spatz."

"I'm glad we rescued him," Oz said. He nudged Caydon. "Hey — what's up?"

Caydon was as still as a statue. His eyes were wide open, yet he looked asleep.

"His shoes!" Lily gasped. "They're GROWING!"

It wasn't just his shoes. Caydon's legs and arms were suddenly the size of trees, and his body grew so massive that he knocked everyone else off the bench. Lily fell awkwardly and banged one of her knees. When the giant Caydon stood up, he was taller than the roof of the bike shelter.

"I know what this is!" Silver cried out. "Stand back — he's having another vision!"

None of the other kids in the playground had noticed that a ten-metre-high boy was looming over them, casting an enormous shadow. It was very odd to see them strolling about normally, within centimetres of his monstrous black school shoes.

"But what's he seeing this time?" Oz asked. "Will we see it too?"

"Watch," Silver said grimly.

Caydon put two fingers to his lips and let out a deafening whistle, so loud and piercing that Oz and Lily

160

covered their ears. Then he roared – in a mighty voice that echoed across Holloway – "STEGGY! HERE, BOY!"

The ground beneath their feet trembled, as if something gigantic was running towards them. Caydon bent down, pulled the concrete bench out of the ground, and hurled it across the playground with a bellow of "FETCH!" The bench smashed against the wall in a shower of splintered wood and broken concrete.

And then the bell rang for the end of break and everything was suddenly back to normal. Oz and Lily found themselves sitting on the bench again, with a normal-sized Caydon sitting between them.

"Are you – OK?" Oz cautiously touched his friend's arm.

"Think so," Caydon gasped. "It wasn't so scary this time – I was just playing with a dog."

"A dog?" Lily rubbed her leg and found that it didn't hurt any more. "Did you see it?"

"No, I woke up too soon, but I could feel it coming towards me."

"I'd better report this to Mum." Silver took her phone from her scruffy backpack and quickly sent a text. The phone bleeped back at her almost at once. When she read it, her face hardened. "There's been a serious incident in Muswell Hill and now they need our reports urgently. Looks like we'll be missing school after all."

16

Steggy

The government car that collected the children just before PE had darkened windows, but it was still possible to see out. The moment they turned into Muswell Hill High Street, it was obvious that the "incident" had been very serious indeed.

"Wow, look at Marks & Spencer," Oz said. "The window's been smashed to pieces! And look at the flower shop!"

"Someone's gone bonkers with a bulldozer." Caydon pressed his face against the window. "It's ripped up all the trees and hedges, crashed into the shops. . ."

"This'll be a tough clear-up job," Silver said. "First they've got to deal with the rubble and broken glass, and then they have to wipe everybody's memory."

The groups of shoppers on the pavements stood very still, like waxworks. Groups of masked police moved among them, spraying them with a mist of aerosol.

There was an SMU police cordon around the unexplained kennels. Silver opened the car window at the checkpoint to show her card.

"You'll have to get out here, Major," the policeman said. "The road's covered with chewed-up trees."

The four of them got out of the car, into a scene of devastation. The entrance to the kennels was now a gaping, jagged hole. The ground was littered with lumps of masonry and concrete, and there was an acrid haze of dust.

"How did this happen?" Lily took Silver's hand fearfully. "A bomb? And what's happened to all the animals? I hope Edwin's OK."

"Of course Edwin's OK," Caydon said scornfully. "He's a ghost!"

"I hate to think of him being frightened, that's all."

"Ghosts don't get frightened."

"How do you know? And he's shy – he might not want to come back."

The reception area of the unexplained kennels was a shambles. The metal door had been thrown right off its hinges; the desk and chairs had been reduced to matchwood. The cage that Edwin liked to haunt had been ripped apart like tissue paper. Far below them, they heard hoots and shrieks from the underground cages.

Two figures in white boiler suits and masks like plastic goldfish bowls were waiting for them. One was J and the other was B62.

"Well, we weren't expecting that," J said. His voice was brisk, but his face was pale inside the mask. "The animals are all under control now, thank goodness, and the clear-up is under way. I shudder to think what this is costing! B62, give the children their suits."

"Yes, sir." She handed them each a baggy white boiler suit and a plastic mask.

"These are to protect you from prehistoric microbes," J said. "When Caydon's whistle sounded, one of our most secret and dangerous creatures suddenly went berserk — it took us by surprise, because he's usually rather quiet."

"What — one creature did all this damage?" Silver gasped. "It must be the size of a double-decker bus!"

Caydon zipped up his white suit. "It's Steggy, isn't it? That was the name I called out in my vision — is he a giant dog, or something?"

"This is strictly classified, and you must never tell a living soul," J said. "But Steggy's not a pet dog. He's a pet dinosaur."

"A real dinosaur?" Oz's heart gave a leap of excitement. A few years ago he'd been mad about dinosaurs, and he had never stopped wishing he could see a real one. "Steggy — that must be short for stegosaurus — wow!"

"I've got a plastic stegosaurus on my bedroom shelf," Caydon said. "But he's only a couple of centimetres tall."

Lily was trying to remember all the different pictures in their old dinosaur book. "It's not the one with the tiny arms and big teeth, is it?"

"No – don't you know anything? That's a T. rex."

"A stegosaurus is herbivore," J said. "It only eats trees and hedges – and window-boxes, and the plants at Marks & Spencer. Don't be alarmed, he's under control now. It took a tank to drag him back when he stopped rampaging."

"But how did he get up to the street?" Oz asked. "Don't tell me he can work a lift – he wouldn't be able to press the buttons."

J said, "He crashed through a network of sewage pipes, using them as a sort of ladder. It's going to be very tricky to put right."

The lift they had used last time was out of action. Once they were all in their protective suits, J and B62 took them to the much bigger lift that was used to move very large unexplained creatures.

"Steggy" was kept at the very deepest level of the secret kennels, a long way below the pavements of Muswell Hill. They came out into a dark corridor, dimly lit with one weak bulb. There was a strong smell – dirty straw and droppings, like a farmyard or a zoo, rotting boiled cabbage and mouldy bread. The idea that they were smelling a genuine dinosaur was incredible. Even Lily was more excited than scared.

They were met by a tall lady, whose thick glasses flashed inside her mask. "Hello, I'm Dr Flanagan, in charge of Steggy's care team. We keep it dark down here because bright light makes him agitated. And I must ask you not to take photographs or make any sudden movements. If he's startled he spits."

"Dinosaur dribble," Caydon said in a dazed voice. "That's the weirdest thing I ever heard! Are we still in my vision?"

"No, this is perfectly real," Dr Flanagan said. "We're at the point where science and magic meet – it's a fascinating area of research."

Lily heard a sound behind them, like someone enormous turning over in bed. She swallowed and grabbed Silver's hand again, but she couldn't resist turning round to look.

Inside the cavernous cage was the black outline of the dinosaur. When Lily's eyes adjusted to the dim light, she saw a huge creature as tall as a bus and twice as long. She made out a tiny head, a great round back and a long tail. From the neck to the end of the tail its spine was studded with thick metallic plates. She was convinced that the dinosaur's little glinting eyes were looking straight at her and she wished they wouldn't.

"Those are his dorsal plates, along his back," Oz whispered. "And those are his tail spikes – he's awesome!"

Behind her mask, Dr Flanagan smiled. "You wouldn't have thought he was awesome when he heard that whistle – he went crazy!"

"Is his skin black?" Oz pressed closer to the thick bars of the cave. "Dark grey?"

"Very dark green," Dr Flanagan said. "With dark red tips on the tail spikes. He's not normally dangerous – he just sits chewing trees all day. We tried to take him out for some exercise on Hampstead Heath once – in the middle of the night, naturally – and all he wanted to do was eat it. So usually he's rather thick and lazy, but when he heard that whistle he suddenly started thrashing about like a mad thing."

"The whistle was me, in my vision," Caydon said.

"Well, you set off all the other unexplained creatures too – I never heard such a racket! And Steggy charged through all the barriers into the high street."

"Anything you can tell us would be helpful," J said. "I'll be the first to admit that we're rather at sea here. That's why I called another emergency scramble."

Caydon said, "It wasn't a scary vision this time. I was a giant – which felt incredibly cool – and I was whistling for my pet. Don't tell me Steggy was ever anyone's pet!"

"The SMU has held Steggy since the Middle Ages," J said. "He's one of our deepest national secrets. Every new monarch or prime minister is told about him, but no one else."

"I didn't know the SMU existed that long ago," Oz said. "It obviously wasn't part of MI6 back then – that didn't exist either."

"Good point, Oz," said J. "When Steggy was found, there was no official protocol for handling the unexplained. They didn't know about dinosaurs and thought he was some kind of dragon."

"And they had to pay witches to wipe people's memories," Dr Flanagan said. "Otherwise it would be all over the history books. Steggy just burst out in Cheapside one day – reducing half of it to rubble – and Henry V's soldiers managed to capture him by making him drunk."

"Wow, talk about a weird job," said Caydon. "How did they do it?"

Behind her mask, Dr Flanagan was chuckling. "According to our secret records, they poured barrels of booze into Steggy's mouth until he fell asleep. Apparently it took most of the alcohol in the City of London, and you could hear his snores in parts of Kent. Nobody knows where he came from, but it was obvious from the start that he had been a pet. He was tame, and he obeyed certain commands like 'Sit' and 'Fetch'. And he obeyed you, Caydon. He thought you were his owner and he smashed half of Muswell Hill trying to get to you."

Caydon did not like the idea of a stegosaurus thinking he owned it. "He's not going to try to follow me home, is he?"

"Not now," J said. "But we need to know who you turned into in your vision. Who did Steggy think you were?"

"I think I had a beard," Caydon said slowly. "And I think I was planning to give my pet a tin bath full of beer."

"Interesting," said Dr Flanagan. "Weak ale is an important part of Steggy's diet – his main source of complex carbohydrates now that the Flatulam Root is extinct."

J sighed. "Very interesting, but it doesn't tell us anything useful."

"Excuse me, sir," Silver said, in her professional voice. "You haven't heard our full report from the Great Fire. Alba said her sons kept going on about a pet of theirs. Could that be Steggy?"

J and B62 didn't often show that they were excited, but now they darted eager glances at each other.

"Thank you, Major," J said. "This could be the best lead we've had in ages. Come to my office and make your full report now. B62, send someone to Skittle Street to fetch the talking animals. And call up the files on all of Alba's sons – human or otherwise."

17

A Useful Cat

The novelty of not being at school had begun to wear off. Lily, Oz and Caydon were starting to worry. Everyone they saw was very cool and professional, yet the atmosphere in the unexplained kennels was tense. While they were eating Marks & Spencer sandwiches (left over from the clear-up) in the conference room, they could hear running feet outside the door, and distant, urgent shouts.

Finally, Silver came back from her reporting, very pale and serious.

"Well?" Oz demanded. "What's going on?"

"I'm not sure." Silver sat down. "They just asked me loads and loads of questions about the witches. I thought we'd foiled Alba's evil plan, but everyone seems to think she's got something else up her sleeve."

Lily asked, "When can we go home?"

"Nobody would tell me. We're on such high alert that I'm not allowed to ring my mum – even though she's my commanding officer."

The man known as J came into the conference room in time to hear this. "She's quite right, I'm afraid. I wanted to avoid using you three again, but you're the carriers and there isn't anyone else."

"Oh." Lily's heart sank. She was longing for home, and the grave look on J's face told her this was going to be dangerous. She felt Oz thinking the same.

"You've got another mission for us?" Caydon said. "Is it time travel again?"

"Possibly – but we're not sure where or when. B62, I'll have a cup of tea and one of those chocolate muffins. We know that Alba wanted to put out the Great Fire so that she could free her sons. She seemed to believe that freeing her sons would give her the power to cast a blight of evil across the land, but we didn't know anything else. Caydon's vision has given us a vital clue." J sat down at the table. "We have files on all eighty-four of Alba's sons. No less than twenty-seven of them were fathered by giants – she liked them big and stupid, as Twelvey said."

"So giants are real as well," Oz said. "And I used to think fairy tales were made up."

"Yes, giants are real, but very rare. And all of them have been under lock and key for hundreds of years."

"I suppose it'd be hard for a giant to live in hiding," Caydon said.

"Precisely — things that big tend to stick out, and they'd all been captured by the end of the ninth century. The problem is that the records are so ancient, nobody remembers exactly where they're locked up, and the keys were lost years ago. Thanks to Caydon's vision, however, we do know which two giants we're looking for."

A picture flashed up on the screen behind him — two painted wooden figures with shaggy brown beards.

"Alba's first two sons were twins named Gog and Magog. They might as well have been called 'Dumb' and 'Dumber'. They're a pair of brutes, but they're vitally important to the survival of London. Though nobody's quite sure why, if Gog and Magog are let loose, the very heart of the city will be destroyed."

A second picture appeared on the screen behind him. It was a London street, with crowds of people and a grand procession of mounted soldiers. In the middle of a sort of carnival float were two-metre-high models of the two giants.

"Every year," J said, "images of Gog and Magog are carried through the City of London at the Lord Mayor's Show, as a symbol of our continuing safety. We know it is Gog and Magog that Alba is looking for."

The picture on the screen changed to a beautiful illuminated manuscript from the Middle Ages. There was a painting of two bearded thugs with a strange green humpbacked dragon that was very like—

"Steggy!" they all cried out together.

"Yes, this picture shows that Steggy belonged to Gog and Magog – we think he might have been a birthday present from their mother."

There was a knock at the door and Rosie from the commando unit came in, with Spike on her shoulder, quivering with excitement.

"Sorry to interrupt, sir," Rosie said. She smiled quickly at the children. "It's Demerara – she's got herself into trouble again."

J let out a great sigh. "What's that ridiculous little cat done now? You'd better bring her in."

"We can't," Spike squeaked. "She's inside that dinosaur you've got in the basement."

"Inside?" Lily jumped out of her chair. "You mean – she's been eaten? But you said Steggy was a vegetarian!"

"Now, don't get into a state," Spike said kindly. "She's immortal, isn't she? So he can't digest her."

"Well, nothing surprises me any more," J said. "How did it happen?"

"She was chasing a rat," Spike said. "Not one of my soldiers – just a normal Muswell Hill rat. I tried to stop her, but she ran after it right down to the dinosaur's cage, fell into his bucket of beer – and he swallowed her by mistake!"

J frowned. "This could be awkward. I've got an

173

important job for Demerara, and she won't be much use if she's inside a stegosaurus. I'd better talk to her."

"Can we come?" Lily asked. "Oh, poor Demerara! She must be so scared!"

Demerara was not scared. J took them all back to Steggy's high-security cage, and the first thing they heard when they came out of the lift was the muffled voice of a cat in a fury.

"This is INTOLERABLE! I insist that you get me out AT ONCE! You have no idea how DISGUSTING it is in here!"

Caydon and Oz were laughing softly.

"It's NOT FUNNY!" thundered the voice of the furious cat. "How would you like to be inside the stomach of a prehistoric beast? It's like swimming around in a huge bowl of really STINKY cabbage soup!"

J said, "Hello, Demerara."

"Is that J? Tell this horrid woman to GET ME OUT OF HERE!"

Dr Flanagan, behind her plastic mask, was frowning. "I've told you – it's out of the question."

"Cut him open!"

"Certainly not," Dr Flanagan said sternly. "For the last time, I am not cutting open a priceless dinosaur! I'm afraid you'll just have to wait until Steggy expels you naturally."

"NO-O-O!" roared Demerara. "I WILL NOT BE A DINOSAUR POO!"

Everyone – except Dr Flanagan – exploded with laughter at this, which made the little cat even more furious.

"Get a big knife and cut me out NOW!"

The dinosaur himself lay like a mountain of rock, his tiny eyes blinking stupidly in the shadows. He didn't seem to know that he had a cat thrashing about inside his stomach – though when she really screeched, his daft face looked faintly puzzled.

Lily pressed her face to the bars of the cage. "Demerara, calm down! It's going to be fine!"

"Fine? His stomach acid has stripped off my claw polish!"

"Hey, Demerara," Oz said. "What's it like in there?"

"Smelly! And there's all sorts of rubbish floating about – pebbles – potted begonias from Marks & Spencer – a skeleton that looks like a kangaroo with wings—"

"So THAT'S what happened to it!" muttered Dr Flanagan.

"And a great big metal key that keeps banging against my bottom."

"A key?" J asked eagerly. "Demerara – this could be one of the most useful things you've ever done! Steggy belonged to Gog and Magog, and I'll bet that's the key to the giants' secret dungeon!" He turned to Dr Flanagan. "If it's in his stomach, why hasn't he – er – expelled it?"

"We're not sure," Dr Flanagan said thoughtfully. "He's

far too big to X-ray properly, but we think there are some things that just stay inside him—"

"Well, I REFUSE to be one of them!" shrieked Demerara. "Get me OUT!"

"She really must come out," J said. "And I need that key."

Dr Flanagan frowned. "I'm sorry, I can't risk harming him. He's one of only three living dinosaurs left in the world – and the two in Russia are only pterodactyls!"

"But there must be some way we can get them out without damaging him."

"Well," Dr Flanagan said slowly, "I suppose I could try to make Steggy burp them out."

"Good idea," J said.

"I warn you, it'll be noisy." Dr Flanagan unlocked the door to Steggy's cage and went in. What happened next was fascinating. She took down a hose that hung on the wall and held the nozzle above a huge tin bucket. A brown, foaming stream of beer gushed into the bucket, filling the cage with its sour, yeasty smell.

Steggy moved his head towards the smell and looked slightly interested. He plunged his dark green muzzle into the bucket of beer and started to drink with gigantic gulping sounds.

"HEY!" screamed a muffled voice from his belly. "What's going on?"

The stegosaurus drained every drop of beer. He lay

back comfortably, and there was a rumble like loud thunder. His mountainous green sides quivered.

Dr Flanagan smiled darkly. "This'll teach that cat to muck about with my best creature!"

"U-R-R-R-GHPP!!!!" Steggy let out a burp so tremendous that everyone's ears rang for half an hour afterwards. A blob of slime shot out of his mouth and hit the wall with a splat. At the same moment there was a ringing sound, and a huge metal key, about half a metre long, landed on the stone floor. It was covered with gooey slime. Dr Flanagan washed it under a tap in the wall and handed it through the bars to J.

"Excellent!" J grasped it triumphantly.

"Demerara!" cried Lily and Silver. "Is she hurt?"

"No harm done." Dr Flanagan picked the shocked, quivering, slimy cat off the stone floor, and held her under the tap. The cat spluttered and coughed, but was too shocked to struggle. "Now take her away." She tore a piece of extra-thick paper towel from an enormous roll in one corner, wrapped Demerara in it, and shoved her into Lily's arms.

"Demerara – are you OK?"

"Did you see that?" hissed Demerara. "She soaked me in freezing cold water and if I wasn't immortal that would probably kill me! J – I think you should FIRE this hard, unfeeling woman."

"And I think," said Dr Flanagan, "that you should keep

177

your SILLIER agents away from my research!"

"Who're you calling SILLY?"

J smiled and reached out to pat Demerara's cross wet head. "You are rather silly – but you've been brilliant today. We might've wasted months searching for this key. Major Biggins, take the carriers back to school – and when you return to Skittle Street, please buy this useful cat a tin of her favourite food."

18

A Defection

"I'm hoping for a normal day today," Oz said. "A nice, boring day without any crazy adventures."

"Me too," Caydon said. "Boredom's a treat after scaredom."

Silver ran her plastic scanner across Lily's cheese and tomato baguette. "OK, you can eat that."

They were in the queue for lunch in the school canteen, the day after their meeting with the leftover stegosaurus. Yesterday afternoon they had gone back to school, and the rest of the day had been totally un-magic.

"Can you scan all my chips at once?" Caydon asked. "Or do you have to do them one by one?"

Silver giggled. "Don't be daft."

The dinner lady serving the chips was a lady called

Maria, a calm person with grey hair, who everyone liked because she was never cross and gave big portions.

Caydon held out his plate to her. "Hundreds of chips, please."

"OK, lovey."

In between scooping up the chips and dropping them on Caydon's plate, something happened to Maria's face — it shrank and hardened, and her greyish eyes darkened to deepest black with depths of red.

The eyes looked intently into Caydon's and his heart somersaulted. He tried to nudge Silver, but he couldn't move or make a sound. The racket of the canteen cut out and a voice spoke, close to his ear.

"Caydon Campbell? Can you hear me? Have I got through?"

Silver's scanner let out an urgent series of bleeps. She moved so quickly that Caydon couldn't work out what she was doing — but suddenly she had a gun and she was pointing it at Maria.

Maria's new face twisted in agony and bitter fury. "Let me go!"

Silver said, "Hallo, Twelvey."

Caydon knew her now. Oz and Lily knew her. The canteen was as still and silent as a stopped film.

"So you thought you'd have another go at kidnapping the carriers," Silver said. "Nice try."

"It's not what you think." Twelvey was shaking inside Maria's overall. "I want to come over to your side."

"Why should we believe that?"

"I can help you. I have vital information about Alba's next move. Please, Silver! I'm doing this for my husband and my daughter!"

"I think she's telling the truth," Lily whispered.

"It's worth the risk if she knows anything about Alba," Silver said. "This could be just the break we need. Listen, Twelvey – we'll meet you out by the bins in five, but no funny stuff. Got that?"

"Thank you! You won't be sorry!"

Twelvey's face sagged and swelled – and suddenly she was Maria again, piling chips on Caydon's plate as if nothing had happened. The racket started again and the children gaped at one another's pale, stunned faces.

"Let's go," Silver said. "Put your trays down and follow me."

Caydon kept hold of his plate of chips and started eating them while Silver was hurrying them all out of the busy canteen, hiding her gun in the droopy sleeve of her jersey. There was a fire door at the side of the school that led to a square of tarmac where the huge dustbins were kept, and where the teachers parked their cars. Silver pushed them all through this door.

"We're not allowed here," Lily said.

A tall, slim woman with black hair stepped out from behind one of the dustbins. It was Twelvey, in a tight, short blue dress.

"Are you alone? Is this a trap?"

"We're not working for your horrible sisters, if that's what you mean," Silver said. "Tell us what you want."

Twelvey glanced round anxiously and lowered her voice. "I want you to arrest me and I'll tell you anything you like. But I must have twenty-four-hour protection, and immunity from prosecution—"

"I don't have the power to promise anything," Silver said. "If you come quietly I'm sure you'll be looked after."

"Hey, I've seen that dress before," Caydon said, still eating his chips. "Ms Gupta was wearing it this morning – I hope you haven't left her naked!"

Twelvey ignored him. She was staring at Silver, her face hungry with hope. "I'll do anything, if you just let me see my husband and daughter. I must be with them to protect them from what is to come!"

"Alba makes all that fuss about her parenting classes," Twelvey said, "and she's the worst parent in the world. She doesn't understand that normal mothers – even wicked ones – will do practically anything to protect their children. That's why I'm here."

The defecting witch had been brought to a secure SMU interrogation suite, in a bunker underneath the MI6 building beside the Thames. Oz, Lily and Caydon watched her warily, waiting for any sign that she might turn dangerous.

But Twelvey was quiet and calm, wearing handcuffs and drinking a mug of tea. She looked at J. "Do you agree to my conditions?"

"I suppose so," J said. "You won't be charged with any D33 crime you tell us about, and you and your family will have round-the-clock security. But I can't just release you straight back into the community. I'm afraid you must have at least a year of Evil Management Classes."

"Oh, great — two hours a week with a load of chain-smoking, recovering demons." Twelvey sighed crossly. "OK."

"Now tell us what we need to know." J held up the huge metal key. "We know that this is the key to the secret dungeon of Gog and Magog."

"Where did you find that?" Twelvey stared at it. "Alba's looked everywhere."

"We also know that Alba wants to free her sons. Because if they stop guarding London, we're all doomed."

"She doesn't care what it takes to get power," Twelvey said. "That's why she thought I wouldn't care about Ludo and Greta. Well, that was her big mistake. I don't give a toot about all the other humans who are going to die in agonies — but these are MY humans!"

Oz and Lily felt each other's fear, but they also felt the comfort of the other voice that had spoken to them when they were little. The magic in the room was very strong, and for a moment Lily had the strangest feeling – that somehow Daisy was looking after them.

J was stern. "Where is the dungeon?"

"I'm surprised you don't know," Twelvey said. "It was your lot that built it. I thought you kept records."

"Many records have been lost."

"The dungeon was such a long way underground that the Great Fire couldn't touch it. After that they built the new place."

"New place?" J asked sharply. "Come on, Twelvey! Where are the giants locked up?"

"Under that vulgar new cathedral."

There was a silence. "You mean," J said, "St Paul's."

"That's not new," Caydon said.

"It's new to her." J was calm, but pale and tense. "The present St Paul's was built at the end of the seventeenth century, after the old one was burned in the Great Fire. You'll understand why Gog and Magog were locked up there when I tell you that the head of the SMU, in the days of Charles II, was a certain Sir Christopher Wren."

"That's the same Sir Christopher Wren who designed the Monument," Silver said. "He also designed St Paul's."

"That's right," said Twelvey. "You see, it all started when Alba found an ancient document at a car boot sale. It said that the king told Sir Christopher to design a new seal for the giants' dungeon – a seal that could never be broken."

"So the seal is somewhere inside St Paul's," Lily said.

Twelvey said, "The seal IS St Paul's. It's the whole building – like an enormous cork in an enormous bottle. Alba knew she'd never shift it. But now she's found another time stitch."

"That's impossible," J snapped. "We've sealed all of them."

The defecting witch smiled nastily. "You don't know about all of them. When the next Great Fire of London came along, St Paul's didn't burn down – but the time fabric was severely weakened. So Alba's planning to slip through the dropped stitch and complete the job by burning the cathedral to the ground and freeing her sons."

"But there hasn't been another Great Fire," Lily said. "She must be lying."

"As a matter of fact," J said, very quietly, "St Paul's Cathedral narrowly missed being burned down on the night of the 29th December, 1940."

"The Blitz," Twelvey said. "A terrible firestorm raged over the City of London, but by some fluke the cathedral was saved."

"It wasn't a fluke!" snapped J. "It was the people of London who saved their cathedral." He turned back to the children. "On the night of December 29th, 1940, German planes dropped thousands of firebombs on the City of London. The firestorm destroyed everything around St

Paul's – but not the cathedral itself. The prime minister, Winston Churchill, sent an urgent order that St Paul's must be saved at all costs. The reason he gave was that it was such a powerful symbol of national pride and hope – but he must have known that Gog and Magog, the Keepers of the Seal, were locked up underneath the place, and that everything would be over for us if they got out."

Twelvey shrugged. "Whatever. Alba says she's going to destroy the cathedral and free her sons. She wants to bond with them, though I think she's left it too late. She fostered them with a family of bears when they were toddlers, and she sent them expensive gifts but never saw them from one birthday to the next. I told you, she's a shocking mother. Much worse than I was. How is Greta, by the way? Any sign of a husband yet?"

"Never mind Greta." J was deeply shaken. He suddenly looked years older. "We need those giants to stay exactly where they are. Doesn't Alba care that she'll be unleashing the forces of darkness?"

"No," said Twelvey. "Alba likes the forces of darkness."

"Luckily, she doesn't have any more of the carriers' DNA," J said thoughtfully. "And without that, the chocolate phoenix is about as much use as a chocolate teapot."

"She'll find some way of getting it," Twelvey said. "She's ever so determined."

"Hang on – that means us, and our DNA," Oz said.

"She'll have to kidnap us again."

"Oh, yes," Twelvey said. "It only went wrong last time because Caydon had that giveaway vision. Next time she won't be stopped by armed commandos."

"Next time they'll have a bodyguard," Silver said, giving the witch a scornful look. "Nobody's going to kidnap the carriers on my watch."

"All the same," J said, "I'll send Elvira to guard the baby."

"Great," Caydon said. "She'll be totally safe with Gran. Look how she dealt with those dryads."

"That was nothing to do with your gran," Twelvey said.

"It was – we all saw her! Lily called her with Silver's bell."

Twelvey let out a sour cackle. "But it wasn't your gran who answered. It was the little walnut tree in the middle of the grove."

"That's what Mrs Fladgate called Daisy!" Lily leapt up excitedly. "Do you mean Daisy drove them away?"

"There's some very old magic around your part of north London," Twelvey said. "It's all tied up with that Roman temple in Seven Sisters. Now I'd like another cup of tea – all this betraying has made me very thirsty."

"All right, you can go now." J nodded to the two armed policewomen waiting beside the door. "Take her to the high-security unit."

"You said I could see my daughter."

"Greta will be allowed to visit you."

"OK." Twelvey was marched out of the room between the two policewomen, still clutching her teacup.

J said, "B62, please put these children into time training right away, and send for the talking animals. I don't want to send them back to 1940, but it's just as well to be prepared."

"Yes, sir — are you all right?"

"Perfectly." He took a deep breath and steadied himself against the table. "It's just that I have rather personal reasons for wanting to keep D33 away from St Paul's."

Everyone was quiet until Lily asked, "Are we going back to school now?"

"No."

"Oh. Are we going home?"

"Not yet, I'm afraid. You're safest here, in the MI6 building."

"Oh."

"Are we staying the night?" Caydon asked. "Do we get government pyjamas?"

J stood up. "Children." He looked at them all in silence for a moment. "This could be the most important job you ever do for your country. If you can't find me when you come back, I want you to go straight to the prime minister and give him the secret code word — cabbage."

They looked at each other doubtfully. Oz said, "Just

'cabbage'? Will he know what it means?"

"He'll know."

"But where will you be?" Lily asked.

"That," J said, "is a very good question. But I'm afraid I can't say more. B62 will take you to the briefing room, where you'll be issued with 1940s clothes, weapons, gas masks and everything else you'll need if you have to make a sudden jump into the past. You never know what Alba's planning to do next."

19

Another Defection

"I'm a key part of this operation," said Demerara.

They found her sitting proudly on the desk, in the bare underground briefing room. Spike was beside her and both were wearing little tin helmets. Oz and Caydon snorted with laughter. Lily and Silver didn't want to offend the animals, but they had to bite the insides of their cheeks to stop themselves giggling.

"In the event of a sudden jump to the past," Demerara went on, "I'm to proceed to St Paul's Cathedral to mould the local cats into an unbeatable fighting machine. You haven't mentioned my hat yet."

"It's lovely," Lily said hastily.

B62 came into the briefing room with a tray of tea, juice and biscuits. "Help yourselves – this is your official snack break." She put the tray down on the desk. "I'll be back in a few minutes."

"Very nice," Spike said, when she had gone. "I'm fond of a digestive." He picked up a biscuit, which looked like a big wheel in his scrawny little paws, and began to nibble at the edges.

"I'll have one of those tasty cheese crackers," Demerara said. "Make that two."

Silver passed the bossy cat some cheese crackers and a saucer of water. The boys had tea and Mars Bars, and Lily chose a glass of fresh pineapple juice.

"What's your special job, Spike?" Caydon asked. "Spike. . .?"

The rat had fallen asleep with his teeth still fastened to the biscuit.

"Spike – what's up with him?" Silver gave the rat a gentle prod, and he collapsed in a little furry, snoring heap.

Demerara gave an enormous cat-yawn. "Dear me, I must lie down—" She curled up on the table, with one cheek resting in the saucer.

From a strange distance, Lily saw that Silver was alarmed, and trying to shake the animals awake. She saw Oz and Caydon yawning, and felt a great wave of sleepiness that made her arms and legs as heavy as stone.

"No!" Silver knocked the glass of juice out of her hand. "Don't drink any more of that!"

Lily wanted to ask "Why not?" but she couldn't drag out the words. She couldn't do anything except collapse on the floor and let the soft darkness wash over her.

Something was tickling Lily's cheek. She brushed it off impatiently, but the tickling went on. She opened her eyes – and was startled to see a furry golden face inches from her own.

"Thank goodness, I think she's awake now," Demerara said. "Are you awake, dear?"

Lily was lying on a cold, clammy stone floor. She heaved herself into a sitting position – her head felt like a cannonball. "What. . .?"

The dirty, miserable faces of Oz and Caydon loomed at her in the darkness. She looked round – not that there was much to look at. They were hunched on the floor of a small cellar, lit by a torch high in the wall, which covered the place with crazy shadows.

"Welcome to the disaster," Caydon said.

"Where's Silver?"

"Dunno. We just woke up here."

"Those drinks we had were drugged," Oz said. "And – you're not going to like this – your hair's been cut off."

"WHAT?" Lily's hands flew to her head – and felt nothing but a centimetre of soft fuzz. Sick with shock, she saw that the boys had also had drastic haircuts.

"Be brave, dear!" Demerara purred kindly into her ear. "Your lovely curls will soon grow back – and it actually looks rather chic!"

"But – where are we? What's going on?"

"You know as much as we do," Oz said. "We fell asleep and then we were here – wherever that is. And we are skinheads."

"We've tried shouting for help," Caydon said.

From somewhere on the floor, Spike's voice cheeped, "We're a long way underground."

A key turned in the door, with a great clanking and grating of metal. Lily, Oz and Caydon huddled together, holding their breath.

And then B62 walked into the cell. Lily sighed with relief. "Oh – this must be part of the special training!"

"Stand up," said B62. "Alba wants to see you."

There was a cold, hard silence, as the terrible truth dawned on them. B62 – J's right-hand woman and the SMU's trusty Miss Moneypenny – was working for the other side.

"It was – you!" Caydon choked. "You're a double agent!"

"Keep your mouth shut," snapped B62. "Don't speak until you're spoken to. Put your hands up where I can see them."

She was holding a gun; they all put their hands up.

"Animals as well," B62 said. "Where's the rat? OW!"

She doubled over to rub her ankle. "He bit me – and now he's run away!"

"Good old Spike!" whispered Oz.

"Silence!" snarled B62. "We'll find him – and even if we don't, one little rat's not going to make much of a difference."

She gestured them out of the cell with the barrel of her gun. Lily, Oz and Caydon walked out into a dark stone corridor, also lit by flaring torches.

Lily was incredibly frightened, and half crazy with worry about Silver. But the feel of Demerara's fur, brushing softly against her legs, reminded her that Silver and the animals were immortal – and Spike had got away. There was still hope.

They stumbled through the darkness for what seemed a long time. Far, far above them, they could hear muffled thuds and thumps.

"In here." B62 opened a door and pushed them all inside.

"Who's this— Oh, the children."

Alba was here, pacing furiously to and fro. The last time they had seen her, she had been wearing a magnificent seventeenth-century gown. She was now wearing a short navy-blue dress with very big square shoulders and dark red lipstick.

"Put them in the corner and keep them quiet," Alba said. "I'll get to them in a minute."

Silver stood in front of the table, her pale face streaked with tears. Her hands and feet were in chains. She was trying to hold her head up proudly, but Lily had never seen her so young and so helpless.

At the table beside Alba sat another sour-faced witch, in a grey jacket and skirt. Lily thought she recognized Secunda, the one who had dressed as a nun during the Great Fire.

"Wait till I get my hands on that Twelvey!" spat Alba. "She always was a turncoat!"

"Never mind about her," Secunda said. "Thanks to B62 we found out just in time and got here first. The fires have started, the bombs are raining down outside, and this place should go up any minute. Did you see those boys of yours?"

"No." Alba was glowering.

"Didn't that key work?"

"The key worked beautifully – but the twins wouldn't let me near them! I just don't understand it. I brought them two lovely dead pigs."

Lily slipped her hand into Oz's, knowing he was thinking the same thing – if Alba's giant sons were here, it meant they were deep underneath St Paul's cathedral. And if the fires had started, it could only mean they'd come back in time to 1940, the height of the Blitz. Whole flocks of butterflies fluttered in her stomach.

"Maybe they'll come out when the cathedral has

burned properly." Secunda sounded impatient. "You should be thinking about how we're going to seize power. Do we let the Germans invade?"

"No," Alba said. "Hitler doesn't deserve it. I say destroy most of them and start with a clean slate. It'll be easy-peasy once I break the seal and free my twins. This was my whole plan, and it seemed so simple — once my boys stop guarding this stupid city I can give all my bad magic free rein. You'd think they'd jump at the chance!"

Secunda sniffed and made a face. "I can smell that perfume again. It's coming off the humans. Can I kill them? You've got enough DNA now."

"I'm going to throw them to the boys," Alba said. "They used to love eating human children."

Lily was in the middle of one of Greta's calming exercises, and nearly squeaked out loud. This mission had turned into a nightmare. They were years in the past, with their bodyguard in chains and no one to protect them. Without taking their eyes off Alba, the twins and Caydon grasped each other's hands.

"What about the vampire and the cat?" Secunda asked.

"I don't know. Lock them in a cell till I make up my mind. Wasn't there another talking animal?"

"A rat." B62 was pale and scared. "He — he escaped."

"That was careless of you," Alba said. "You'd better find him — or you know what I'll do."

"Yes, Alba," whispered B62.

"Now take them away."

B62 bent down to pick up Demerara – who instantly bared her teeth and hissed.

"Listen to me, talking cat," Alba said. "The next time you do that, I will personally pick you up and hurl you across this room. I will break all your bones – and then I'll tie you up so the bones mend in the shape of a pretzel."

"No!" cried Lily.

"Let her pick you up. Don't make trouble," Silver told Demerara quietly.

"Well said, vampire-girl." Alba gave her a sneering smile. "You should think about coming to work for D33 – I've got several of the undead on my payroll."

Demerara closed her mouth and allowed B62 to pick her up. With her free arm, B62 tugged at the chain around Silver's hands.

Silver looked at Lily and mouthed, "Be brave!"

"Lily – my darling!" Demerara screwed up her green eyes and burst into loud, mewing tears. "Be brave – and don't be frightened by this HORRIBLE woman whose dress is much too tight round the bum!"

Secunda gave a snort of laughter.

"CURSE your feline IMPERTINENCE!" screamed Alba. "B62 – take them away!"

"Yes, ma'am." She hurried them out of the room.

"And that lipstick does NOTHING for you!" Demerara spat, just before the door shut.

Lily swallowed hard. It felt horribly lonely and un-magic without Demerara and Silver.

"Your frock is rather tight," Secunda chuckled. "You never will admit you're really a size fourteen."

"Shut up! I'm a perfect twelve. Now help me drag the kids to the dungeon. I do hope the boys like them!"

The two witches marched the children from the room, through a long corridor, and down a flight of stone steps. These steps came out into a great, bare stone cave, with rough stone walls. The uneven floor was wet and slippery.

Alba produced the key that had been in Steggy's stomach. She unlocked a thick iron door. A smell wafted out of it, of dirty straw and rotting food. It was very warm.

"Boys!" Alba called into the gloom. "Mummy's back! Come and see the lovely treat I've brought you!"

One by one, she shoved the children into the giants' dungeon and slammed the door behind them.

20

Food for Giants

They were in an enormous dungeon, as big as the cathedral itself, lit by flaring, sputtering torches high in the stone walls. Electricity didn't seem to reach this far below the pavement.

"Wow, I can see you properly now," Caydon told Lily. "Your head's a really funny shape without that big puff of hair."

She turned on him crossly. "We're about to be eaten by giants and all you can do is say mean things about my head!"

"Sorry – OK? Actually I think it looks quite nice."

Oz gazed around the vault of shadows. "Where are the giants? I thought we'd be in their mouths by now."

"All I can see is two big black heaps over in the corner," Lily said. "I think they're coal or something."

"BOYS!" screamed Alba's voice, on the other side of the door. "Look what Mummy's found for you this time – real human children! Now why don't you gobble them up and blast your way out of this SILLY PRISON?"

The two black heaps shifted – they were not heaps of coal. Lily gasped and tried to duck behind Oz. With a great noise of grunting and heaving, Gog and Magog crawled out of the darkness.

Lily, Oz and Caydon had seen some amazing things during their adventures with the SMU, but this was truly extraordinary. They were looking at real giants, like the giants you read about in fairy tales – huge, bearded men as big as buildings, with massive arms and legs and enormous dumb heads. Their vast faces were crude and lumpy; their eyes were deeply stupid.

The children clung together and froze, as the stupid eyes of the giants stared at them. One of them put out a huge finger and touched the top of Caydon's head.

"Ow!" Caydon muttered.

"Well, hurry up and eat them – I haven't got all day!" shouted Alba's voice. "Don't just PLAY with your food!"

The twin giants suddenly raised their great shaggy heads and roared with all their might. They stamped their feet and rattled their thick chains until the earth shuddered — and a monstrous hairy hand sent the children flying across the room.

They landed in a bruised heap, just inside the door. "Drat," said Alba. "I was sure this would work. They used to love eating mashed children!"

"Perhaps they'll fancy them later," Secunda's voice said. "Now come on, Alba — the firestorm's going beautifully, but St Paul's hasn't caught yet."

"We can't do a thing with this city unless my twins stop guarding it! Oh, I suppose you're right — I can come back when it's all in ashes. I didn't think it would be this difficult."

"I keep telling you," Secunda said. "Londoners are a lot cleverer than you think."

"Nonsense — they're completely DRIPPING WET. No wonder I can't start my damned fire!"

There was a sound of footsteps, then silence.

Oz, Lily and Caydon slowly sat up, rubbing their bruised knees and elbows.

Lily said what they were all thinking. "Now what do we do?"

"We look for a way out," Caydon said. "If we just sit here we'll go crazy."

"But what way out? We're miles underground — we'll never get that door open."

"Maybe there's another door," Oz said. "Or an air vent we can get into." He and Caydon began to crawl along the rough stone wall on their hands and knees, desperately feeling for any kind of opening.

"It's no good — this is the worst thing that's ever happened to us, and we'll never get out!" Lily sniffed and wiped her eyes with the sleeve of her jersey. "Even if those things don't eat us, we'll probably die of hunger—"

"Shhh!" Caydon hissed suddenly. "Listen!"

Beneath the huffing of the giants, there was a sound of scratching that got louder and louder. The heaps of straw around the giants began to rustle, and a stream of small black shapes trotted out across the stone floor.

"Ugh!" Lily cowered against the wall. "Rats!" She shuddered as dozens of them ran over her legs, leaving a black smear on her jeans. "They're filthy!"

"That's because we're all covered with soot," a familiar voice squeaked.

"Spike — mate!" Caydon's face lit up as he grabbed the rat on his shoe. "How did you get in here? Wow, it's so great to see you!"

"That's not me," Spike said. "That's just an ordinary one."

"Oops!" Caydon dropped the ordinary rat. "I wish you guys didn't all look the same!"

"*You* know me, don't you, Lily-girl?" Spike hopped on to her arm, and they all got a proper look at his dirty, friendly little face. "Sorry about the soot — we were all running away from the fire."

They remembered now that a great fire was raging far above their heads.

Oz asked, "Has the cathedral caught yet?"

"No – that's the good news." Spike wiped his paws on Lily's sleeve. "But the fire's raging out of control and we've come to get you before it's too late."

This was the first spark of hope since B62 had drugged them and taken them back to the past.

"But we're locked in," Oz said. "And Alba took the key."

"Locks and keys don't bother us rats," chuckled Spike. "We can work our way through pretty well anything. Sit tight and we'll soon have you out of here."

Lily, Oz and Caydon looked at one another doubtfully, not daring to hope it could be this simple.

Lily asked, "What about the giants?"

"Ignore them," Spike said cheerfully. "They haven't even noticed us."

It was true that Gog and Magog seemed totally unaware of the hundreds of wriggling rats, which covered the floor like an unsavoury black carpet. One of the giants picked something out of the straw – a dead pig, which he flipped casually into his mouth. They all winced to hear the crunching of bones between his enormous teeth.

"Lovely manners," Spike said. "They make us lot look quite refined. Lily – do you mind if I get up on your head, love? I have to get the lads in order."

"Go ahead. My hair won't get in the way now."

Lily felt Spike's sharp little paws scramble up her arm and on to the top of her shorn head. Then he stood up on his back legs and let out a serious of sharp, rhythmic cheeps. The army of rats cheeped back, and began to form themselves into separate groups.

"We hang out in tribes, us rats," Spike explained. "These lads here are from Blackfriars Bridge; these here are from the sewers under Cornhill; this crowd here are from the Bank of England, and that lot are from the old synagogue in Bevis Marks. Mostly locals – but I've called them in from all over London."

"I've just thought of something weird," Oz said. "This is 1940, and you were alive then – I mean, you're alive right now over in Skittle Street. What happens if you answer your own call and meet yourself?"

"I don't think that's possible," Spike said comfortably. "For one thing, I remember exactly what I was doing on the 29th December 1940 – and I wouldn't have been any use to anyone. A crate of beer smashed outside the pub in Pooter Street, and us rats had a big party in the nearest drain."

"You were drunk," Caydon said.

"Not half," Spike chuckled. "Old Demerara was furious! Now, you lot get over by the wall, away from the door." He let out another series of squeaks.

Oz, Lily and Caydon moved away from the door as

a black ribbon of rats streamed across the floor. It was fascinating – and a little creepy – to see the efficient way the rodents worked together. They formed themselves into a sort of furry rope up to the keyhole; more rats climbed up the rope and began to nibble – it was like hearing dozens of little fretsaws.

"I didn't know you guys could nibble through locks," said Oz.

"Not always, but this old metal's easy – nice and chewy."

"But we can't let the giants out," Lily said. "They'll escape."

"Don't worry, Lily-girl," Spike said. "They won't notice it's open. And they couldn't fit through this door – the witches are waiting for them to smash their way out!"

"Where are the witches anyway?" she asked.

"We don't have any weapons this time," Caydon added, "real or magic. We can't do anything if they catch us."

"Those old bags are busy spreading the fire. They won't be back for ages."

There was a loud snapping noise, followed by a long, creaking groan as the door of the dungeon swung open.

Lily's heart was beating hard. She looked uncertainly at the boys. "Is it safe, do you think?"

"Of course it's not safe," Caydon said. "But anything's better than being stuck in here – come on."

"We'll go first," Spike said.

"But we can't leave yet!" Lily was anxious. "We have to find Silver and Demerara!"

"All part of the plan." Spike squeaked again. He jumped off Lily's head and swept through the door on the black tide of rats.

Lily, Oz and Caydon hurried after him, though it was impossible to tell which rat he was since he'd lost his tin helmet. The rats seethed and swirled over their feet and around their ankles.

"This is like wading through a sea of dirty fur," Oz said. "Do you know where their cell is?"

"Luckily for us they're not in a cell," Spike said. "Alba chucked them in a bucket of the giants' leftovers."

He whisked round a corner and stopped in front of a row of huge tin buckets, each one as big as the massive metal bins at school.

"Demerara! Can you hear me, old girl?"

"Spike! I never thought I'd be so glad to hear your vulgar little voice! It's perfectly ghastly in here — everything's dead, except Silver, and she won't stop crying, poor dear!" The cat's voice had a ghostly echo inside the bin. "Are the children still alive?"

"Hi, Demerara," Lily called. "We're all fine. Silver, can you hear me?"

Caydon reached up to grasp the edge of the bucket. "Give me a hand — we can tip it over."

The bucket was heavy, but not full. With a lot of

pulling and shoving the three of them managed to heave it over on its side.

Demerara shot out first, a shuddering streak of filthy golden fur. Lily was too happy to see her to care about the muck, and bent down to sweep the cat into her arms.

Silver crawled out more slowly. Her face was swollen with tears and smeared with dirt, but she was making a mighty effort to be stern and professional.

"Nice work, Spike."

"Thanks, Major."

"Silver?" Lily gently touched her arm. "Are you OK?"

"No," Silver said. "This is the worst mess-up of my life. And it happened because I made one stupid mistake."

"But this isn't your fault – you couldn't have known about B62."

"You don't understand." Her lips quivered. "It happened because I forgot that I wasn't just an ordinary eleven-year-old girl. You see, you lot are my first friends for more than two centuries. And I let my guard slip – I didn't scan those snacks. If I'd done that one thing, I could have fought off B62!"

21

The Password is "Cabbage"

Silver sobbed quietly. Lily put an arm around her and Demerara rubbed against her leg. Oz and Caydon were embarrassed and uncertain.

After a long stretch of silence, Spike said, "Well, it looks pretty hopeless – but that's no reason to give up."

Silver wiped her face with one rainbow sleeve. "We might as well give up. I don't know how to get us back to our own time. I don't know any of the SMU contacts here. Alba will destroy the cathedral – which will destroy London—"

"She hasn't done it yet!" Spike squeaked. "And we can still fight her. We can help the people of London who are guarding this place. They don't know anything about giants or witches. They're fighting for the cathedral because of what it means. If London came in a box, St Paul's would be the picture on the lid! I'm not letting it burn down, and I know all my troops feel the same. Isn't that right, lads?" He added a series of sharp cheeps, and the carpet of rats broke out in a squeaking chorus.

"Bravo, Spike, I didn't know you could make such a stirring speech," said Demerara. "I promise to stop killing rats until this crisis is over, and I'll tell the local cats to lay off too. This is a case of all hands – and paws – to the pump."

Lily had been in a fog of despair since waking up down in the underground prison, and for the first time her spirits lifted; it was good to think they could still do something useful.

"You two are much better agents than I am," Silver said. "You're quite right. There's plenty we can do – like keeping out Alba, for a start." She stood up, absently brushing down her filthy clothes. "Spike, do your guys know the way out of here?"

"Leave it to us, boss!"

The tide of sooty rats carried them along twisting stone corridors to the spiral stone staircase that led up to the cathedral crypt. It was a very long way up and Silver, with her superhuman strength, carried Lily and Demerara part of the way.

As they climbed upwards, the distant crashes and bangs grew louder. Bombs were raining down above them and there was a sound like a crowd roaring. The air was bitter and made their eyes sting.

The rats stopped in front of a wooden door. Silver had to struggle through a wriggling duvet of sooty fur to open it.

Finally they came out into a large cellar that was bathed in strange orange light. It took Lily a moment to realize that the light came from two small, high windows, and it was orange because a mighty fire was burning outside.

Like black water trickling away, or iron filings being drawn off by a magnet, the army of rats scattered and disappeared.

"Come on, old girl," Spike said. "I told my lot to gather in the nearest sewer."

Demerara sighed and rolled her emerald eyes. "I was hoping I'd seen the last of sewers!"

"Wait," said Lily. "If you two go off, how will we find you again?"

"Just tell the nearest rat, dear," said Demerara. "The little beasts are horribly good at communication."

The two animals scuttled away into the shadows. Oz, Lily and Caydon looked at Silver.

"You're in command," Oz reminded her. "What do we do now?"

"OK." Silver frowned, trying to think. "Let's get upstairs."

Her vampire's eyes worked well in the dark, and she

quickly made out a door in the far wall, which led to another stone staircase.

"My legs hurt," Lily said. "This is worse than when Dad made us climb that hill in the Lake District."

The door at the top of the stairs was dusty and warped with age. Silver broke the mouldy iron lock.

A rush of smoke made them all (except Silver) burst out coughing. The door was set low into the north wall of the cathedral – and they had stepped out into a firestorm. The cathedral was surrounded by towering walls of flames. Everything, as far as they could see, was burning. Whole buildings blazed; they saw hundreds of firemen bravely trying to fight the fire, but their hoses might as well have been water pistols; a rough December wind fanned the monstrous flames, and this was what made the roaring sound. Planes droned above them; bombs crashed down around them; anti-aircraft guns boomed and pounded.

The air was filled with a fiery shower of sparks, and it was hot in their chests when they tried to breathe. Rasping and spluttering and coughing, they cowered against the soot-blackened walls of the cathedral.

"Back inside!" shouted Silver. She grabbed Lily's jersey and pulled her into the cathedral, while Oz and Caydon wrestled with the wind to shut the door.

"Well, if this place catches, we're toast," Oz said. "Literally."

"It hasn't caught yet." In the half light Silver's face was stern. "Follow me."

She was a professional bodyguard again, instead of a frightened girl. Lily was glad to obey orders and stumble after her through the shadows. The three of them were quiet now, wincing and trembling at the sounds outside.

"This place is huge," Oz said. "Did we come to this bit on our school trip?"

"I did," Caydon said. "We came down to a sort of cellar to see someone's funeral carriage."

"We're in the crypt," Silver said. "I'm going to get us into the cathedral – the local SMU contact will probably be guarding the main door."

"But it's 1940," Oz said. "They won't recognize your card."

"I'll have to use the emergency code."

"What do we do then? Will they be able to get us back to our own time?"

"Frankly, I don't know," Silver said. "But we can still do the job we were sent here to do. Which is to stop St Paul's burning down."

Lily felt another twitch of hope. Surely someone in the SMU could help them, even in 1940.

"Shhh!" They had walked into another stone chamber, where a faint light was showing behind a distant door. Silver put her finger to her lips. Despite the crashing bombs and collapsing buildings outside, this was a chamber of echoes, where the smallest footstep resounded like a gunshot. The door ahead of them stood slightly open. The four of them huddled together to look through the crack.

It was a bare room, furnished with a long table, covered with large rolls of paper. A single electric light bulb dangled above it. There were two people in the room – a skinny young man in a tweed jacket and thick glasses, and a woman in a nurse's uniform.

"No," the young man was saying. "These are classified documents and I won't let you touch them. I don't know why, but I don't like the look of you at all!"

The nurse turned her face towards the light – and they all drew in sharp breaths.

"Get out of my way, you little pipsqueak," Alba said. She took something from the pocket of her starched apron and hurled it at the young man. He crumpled to the floor, totally unconscious.

"At last!" muttered Alba. "This whole operation has been a disaster from start to finish – but now I have Wren's plans!"

She began to rustle impatiently through the rolls of paper on the table. The four children watched her, barely daring to breathe.

"Bum!" spat the witch. "I can't make it out – all these lines and bits of squiggly writing!" She hurried away into the darkness, leaving the plans on the table.

When they were sure Alba had gone, they crept into the room. "Well, we've found our SMU man," Silver said. "Poor guy – he did his best."

Lily looked at the white face of the young man, who lay so still, his glasses hanging off one ear. "Is he dead?"

"No, she only stunned him." Silver knelt down beside him and gently shook his shoulder.

The young men blinked several times and shakily sat up. "H-hello." He gazed around at them all uncertainly. "What on earth's going on? Did something fall on my head?"

Silver took a deep breath. "I haven't got my SMU card," she told him, "because I've come from the future. But my name is Major Silver Biggins – and the password is 'cabbage'."

The young man looked baffled. "What?"

"You must have concussion," Silver said. "Cabbage!"

"What?"

"You're the SMU agent here, right? Or you wouldn't have recognized Alba."

"Sorry, I don't know what you're talking about," the young man said. "I'm not any sort of agent. I'm an architect."

"Architect?" Now it was Silver's turn to look baffled.

"Yes, a whole lot of us volunteered as fire watchers at the cathedral. We've studied the structure and know where the danger points are." He suddenly scrambled to his feet. "The plans! That ghastly nurse was trying to steal them!"

Caydon said, "It's OK, she didn't take them — she couldn't understand them."

"I bet it was something to do with the giants," Lily said. "If she goes back to their dungeon she'll see we've escaped."

"Giants?" The young man stared at them. "You can't play games here, you know. You children should be in an air-raid shelter. Good heavens, my head feels odd!"

"He's not our man," Silver said. "He's an ordinary guy with a gift for spotting witches — if we weren't in the past, I'd recommend him to the recruitment bureau."

The young man straightened his glasses and began checking the great rolls of paper. "It's the incendiary bombs — do you know about those? They're quite small, and when they fall, they fizz for a couple of minutes and then suddenly burst into flames. That's how this dreadful firestorm started. The top skin of the dome here is made of lead. If an incendiary bomb falls on it, the lead will melt and the bomb will drop through the supporting beams, which are made of wood. So that's why we've put fire watchers up there. If they act fast enough, they can pick up the bomb and put it out in a bucket of sand. And if a bomb gets through the lead, we architects will hopefully know where to find it. I was on my way to the roof when that nurse came in."

"We'll come up with you," Silver said. "If that's the weakest spot, that's where Alba will be."

"Look here," the young man said, "I can't allow you children anywhere near the dome!"

Silver ignored him. "Show me those plans."

The young man sighed but gave in. "This one's a cross-section of the dome." He unrolled it on the table. "Incredible, don't you think? There are three layers; it's the first triple dome ever to be built. When this cathedral was opened for business in 1697, it was a miracle of engineering. The cross at the summit is three hundred and sixty-five feet above the pavement! But you lot really can't go up there – it's far too dangerous. I'd better hand you over to a policeman."

"Stay very still, please, or I shall be forced to use a disabling spell."

The thin, papery voice came from the doorway behind them. They all spun round, sure they were about to see another member of the dreadful D33.

But it was a tiny shrivelled old man with white hair, dressed in a peculiar long black coat and a white collar. And though his expression was stern, it was not wicked.

The young man addressed him. "I'm one of the fire watchers. I've no idea what these kids are doing here."

The shrivelled old man looked at Silver. "You're a vampire. Who said you could shelter here?"

"YOU'RE the SMU agent!" Silver cried. "I haven't

got my card – but we've come from the future and the password is 'cabbage'."

"Not this silly game again," sighed the young man.

"Cabbage?" the little old man repeated. "Yes, my dear – I do indeed represent the SMU. Follow me, and you can brief me on the way."

He turned around and walked straight through the wall.

A second later, he came back. "Sorry – I forgot you weren't ghosts."

The eyes of the young man were huge with astonishment. "Please don't faint," Silver said. "We haven't time."

"Faint? I have no intention of fainting!" The young man grinned. "If this is a dream, it's the best one I've had in years. I had always hoped ghosts and vampires were real!"

22

Showdown

"Well, well!" The ghost's wrinkled face creased into a kindly smile. "When this crisis is over, I must mention you to the recruitment bureau! What's your name?"

"Newton," the young architect said. "Andrew, not Isaac. My friends call me Newt."

"How do you do? I'm the ghost of the Reverend Silas Prout, and I've been the SMU agent here since I died back in 1921. Let's all introduce ourselves, shall we?"

Everyone said their name and Newt shook hands with all of them, except Mr Prout.

"I can't shake hands these days," said the reverend. "I simply haven't the cells." He looked over the rims of his ghostly glasses at Silver. "My dear, I know the treatment of vampirism has come on in leaps and bounds, but unfortunately, some of our statues are still very set in their old ways. There may be a bit of trouble."

Silver nodded miserably. "Don't worry, I can take it."

"He must mean they'll shout at her," Caydon said. "Like the gargoyles at my church."

"Good grief!" whispered Newt.

Lily couldn't imagine being shouted at by a statue, and was rather curious to see it, but she felt deeply sorry for Silver. "Don't listen to them!"

"Quite right," Mr Prout said. "You must remember that we're all on the same side, trying to save this precious building from the flames. That witch you saw smuggled herself into St Paul's inside the body of a nurse. I knew something was wrong when the poor girl woke up nude beside the tea urn in the crypt."

"Alba's trying to free the giants," said Silver.

"So it's Alba again, is it? Those frightful daughters of Diocletian are a constant thorn in the side of the department."

"Diocletian?" Newt echoed faintly. "Good grief!"

The old ghost said, "Mr Newton, you have entered the realm of the unexplained; nothing is surprising here. We need you to stop being amazed and guide us through the inner workings of the dome."

"Righto!" Newt returned to the table and gathered an armful of the rolled-up plans. "I'll save my amazement for later. It's just that I didn't think a bit of routine fire watching was going to be so fascinating!"

"It's a shame none of you can walk through walls. I'll have to take you the long way round."

The Reverend Mr Prout was a calm old ghost, and they were all glad to let him lead them out of the crypt into the magnificent main body of the cathedral – it was a shock to remember how beautiful it was. But just outside the windows, the flames towered and crackled and roared, and everything inside was bathed in an orange glow.

Oz asked, "We're not too late, are we?" He was wondering how on earth they were ever going to escape from here – the time and the place – even if they did stop Alba destroying St Paul's.

Lily was thinking the same thing. "If we die now, does it mean we won't get born in the future?"

"Maybe we'll die and get born again," Caydon suggested. "And then die again."

Newt looked over his shoulder. "I say, are you lot really from the future? This is all getting stranger by the minute!"

There was a wooden sign to the "Whispering Gallery", the place in St Paul's dome where you were supposed to be able to hear the smallest whisper from someone on the other side. Lily and Oz had been up here with their primary school class.

"More climbing," Caydon said. "If we ever get back to our time, we're going to be super-fit."

"I've forgotten how many steps there are," Oz panted behind him. "It feels like a million!"

At the very top of the steps, Silver took Lily's hand. "Try not to be scared."

They walked out of the low door on to the dome of St Paul's. Lily's heart flipped as she found herself hundreds of metres above the pavement, surrounded by a sea of fire as far as the eye could see. Planes droned above them; bombs rained down around them; far below on the pavement, hundreds of firemen bravely fought the flames.

There were other people up here already – a handful of men in tin helmets, armed with long black shovels. Newt immediately grabbed a shovel and a bucket of sand and ran to join them. Several bombs fell on the dome. The fire watchers hurried to scoop them up before they burst into flames and burned through the lead.

Oz said, "Where's the shouting coming from?"

Underneath the sound of the bombs and the firestorm, there was a sound like an angry football crowd. It came from below them, and as it grew nearer the voices became more distinct:

"BOG OFF, VAMPIRE!"

"GET THE VAMPIRE, BOYS!"

"VAMPIRE ALERT!"

"Look!" Oz yelled. "I don't believe it!"

This was an incredible sight — four large, sooty statues of saints and apostles, dressed in sooty carved robes, were heaving their stone bodies up on to the dome.

"Ignore them," Silver snapped. "They can't hurt me. It's just the way they're programmed."

"VAMPIRE!" The voices of the statues were a gravelly roar. Tiny chips flew off their great stone sandals as they advanced across the lead roof towards Silver and the three carriers.

"That's quite enough of that!" The ghost of Mr Prout was suddenly standing in front of them. "For the last time, this vampire is on our side! Now, get back to your posts!"

The statues mumbled and rumbled, and then slowly and sulkily climbed back over the low railing. Caydon leant over to take in the extraordinary, mind-boggling sight as they hopped down the great soot-streaked facade of the cathedral and on to their plinths.

"That's terrible!" he said. "Saints are supposed to be good!"

"They're not real saints," Silver said. "They're statues. And they'd be more useful if they could sniff out Alba, instead of wasting time yelling at me."

An incendiary bomb whistled past them. Lily shrieked, but Silver caught it neatly with one hand and blew it out like a birthday candle.

"Wow!" Caydon gasped. "In case we die before I get

a chance to say it – Silver Biggins, you are the coolest bodyguard ever!"

Silver shot a grin at him. "Thanks."

"Doesn't it hurt?" Oz grabbed her hand, in time to see the black burn-mark fade into nothing.

"No. There are some advantages to being a vampire. Now you three try to keep out of the way – I'll help the fire watchers."

Lily asked, "How do you know we're in the right place? Shouldn't we go back inside?"

"This is the weak spot," Silver said. "Alba will try to set fire to the dome – and we'll be ready for her—" She leapt into the air to catch another bomb. "Gotcha!"

But this time, she couldn't blow it out. The bomb fizzed in her hand, and suddenly burst out in searing white flames so bright and hot that Silver dropped it.

The flames swelled into a tall column that grew flaming arms and legs – and finally turned into the figure of a woman.

"Alba!" said Silver. "Get behind me, Lily – she can't hurt me."

The wicked head of D33 was horribly triumphant. The fiendish glint in her smile curdled Lily's blood. She had discarded her stolen nurse's uniform and was now wearing a black boiler suit, rather tight across the hips. In one hand she clutched something gold.

Oz said, "Hey – that's the chocolate phoenix!"

"Quite right, human child," Alba said. "And I'm not

hanging around. The minute I get my poor twins, I'm going to begin a time-travel killing spree that'll make the Black Death look like a school picnic!"

Despite being in the middle of an extremely noisy and highly dangerous nightmare, none of the three carriers could help staring at the golden bird in Alba's hand. There was something hypnotic about the unearthly light that glowed from its dazzling feathers, so beautifully carved by the evil genius Isadore Spoffard.

"Don't waste my time, vampire girl!" Alba shouted. "You can't stop me! In just a moment, I shall peel the lead off this precious dome, as easily as if I were peeling the foil off a pot of yoghurt! Then the seal will be broken and I can get my hands on my sons."

Oz had decided ages ago that they were all going to die, and this made him reckless. "What if your sons don't want to come?"

"What? What did you say?" Alba turned a face of fury towards him. "Of course they do!"

"If they wanted to, they could've smashed their way out by now."

"They're too stupid!" snapped Alba. "That's why they need ME!"

She placed the chocolate phoenix on her arm; it raised its crested head and its beak fell open, and Caydon cried, "It's melting!"

But the golden bird opened a pair of shimmering wings,

let out a cough – UGH! – and a great spark jumped out of its burnished beak.

"My vision!" choked Caydon. "That's what it did in my vision!"

The spark flew up and lodged itself in the lead cover of the dome, just out of reach above their heads.

"Don't bother to put that one in a sand bucket," Alba said. "You'll be wasting your time. Total destruction is mine at last. Boys, Mummy's coming!"

She vanished.

The spark in the dome grew bigger and redder. The chocolate phoenix let out a hoarse cry and hurled itself into the flames – slicing into the lead like a golden bullet and leaving a blazing hole behind it.

And suddenly, they knew they were inside a moment where time flips and another path of reality opens up.

"Stand back, Lily." Silver shoved Lily aside and scrambled up the dome to the blazing hole in the lead.

"No!" Lily screamed up at her. "It's too dangerous!"

"I say—" Newt had climbed round the rim of the dome to join them, and he looked horrified. "You can't let that child in there! How did she get up there, anyway?"

"It's because she's a vampire," Oz said. "She's good at jumping."

The young architect hardly seemed to hear them. "She doesn't know her way—" He glanced round wildly. "Give me a leg-up – I'm going in after her!"

Oz and Caydon managed to grab his legs and shove him up towards the hole in the lead. It was a narrow gap, but luckily Newt was skinny. He dived into it head-first, and a moment later his pale face appeared inside a ring of fire.

"I can't see where the bomb went," he shouted down at them. "But it's left a big black scorch mark – I'm going to follow it as far as I can."

"Come on, help me up," Caydon said. "If I'm going to die because of a magical fireburst I want to see it happening!"

"No!" Lily shrieked.

"I think we have to," Oz said. "I think that's why we're here." He heaved Caydon up to the hole in the dome. "You can stay here on your own if you like – but you know we work better as a threesome."

"You push her and I'll pull her," Caydon shouted. "Hurry!"

"Wait – stop – ow—"

After a lot of frantic pushing and pulling, the three carriers were inside the dome of St Paul's, clinging to a huge wooden beam, part of a web of joists like the bottom of an upside-down ship. It was very dark, but a faint light shone ahead of them. Newt and Silver were already crawling along the broad wooden beam towards it.

"Fire!" Lily wailed. "We're too late!"

23

Rule One for Bodyguards

A cold, hard hand suddenly grabbed Lily's neck from behind.

"Yes – you're far too late," a voice hissed in her ear. "Did you think you could stop me again?"

Lily was so shocked that she couldn't scream. She felt the iron hand clenching the back of her jersey and lifting her off the wooden joist. The dark and cobwebby space was getting lighter by the minute. Just ahead of them Lily saw the chocolate phoenix glowing like an eerie golden lamp, framed by orange flames and angry red sparks.

"Pity I had to cut off your hair," Alba said. "It's hard to get a grip on you now you're nearly bald."

In a trance of fear Lily looked down and saw her trainers dangling in mid-air; she was being carried over the heads of the others, and she saw Silver – who was nearest to the phoenix – trying to shield Newt with her skinny eleven-year-old body.

"I say," the young architect muttered to himself. "It's that horrid woman again. This is a most extraordinary hallucination."

"Put her down, Alba," said Silver. "Let the mortals go."

"Well?" the voice of Secunda asked impatiently, from somewhere in the shadows. "Is it over yet? You said we'd be finished by now – I have theatre tickets."

"For the last time, I have to stay here until I can get at my boys!"

"Face it," Secunda said crossly, "they don't want to come with you. They don't even like you."

"How dare you!" Alba thundered. She dropped Lily, who fell on the broad joist at her feet.

"You said we'd be ruling the world by now. You said I could have France."

"Oh, stop whining – you'll get your weekend in Paris! Now dispose of the mortals."

There was an intense smell of burning, but the flames around the phoenix did not give off smoke. Lily dared to move back a metre or so and take Silver's freezing hand. Silver gave her a reassuring squeeze and she felt the magical power humming through her and Oz and Caydon.

Secunda sat down. "Oof, my poor feet! I don't see why I should do all the dirty work – and I can't understand why it's taken you such an age to defeat a bunch of children and a juvenile vampire. You were totally wrong about the people of London; their annoying bravery and cleverness is making this job well nigh impossible."

"Oh, shut up! B62, I'm leaving you in charge of the phoenix – and killing the mortals."

The woman they knew as B62 was horribly familiar in her modern clothes. She avoided looking at the children. "Can't we just leave them to burn with the cathedral?"

"This is UNBELIEVABLE!" snapped Alba. "I have to do everything myself!" She grabbed Lily and shook her roughly by the scruff of her jersey. "I'll show you lazy cows how it's done!"

"Leave her alone!" Silver, with her superhuman vampire strength, whipped Lily out of Alba's grasp. "You'll have to get past me first."

Alba laughed nastily. "Not so fast, dear – not unless you're prepared to keep Rule One!"

"Of course I'll keep it!" Silver said, scowling.

"Really? Are you sure you wouldn't rather have a nice job on my staff, like B62 here?"

"NO!"

"Seriously, nobody keeps Rule One – why don't you just ignore it?"

"What's she talking about?" Oz hissed. "What's Rule One?"

"It's the first rule of the SMU bodyguard's charter," Silver said. Her face was old and sorrowful, and the flames gleamed on her pointed vampire teeth. "To put the life of the person you're guarding before your own."

"It's rather an easy vow to make when you're one of the undead," Alba said. "You can't be shot or burned or stabbed or blown to smithereens. But there is a way of getting rid of you." She reached up to the mighty wooden joist over her head and casually ripped off a long, jagged splinter.

A vampire, the three carriers remembered, could only be destroyed by a wooden stake driven into its heart.

"No – no, please!" Lily choked.

"I'm so sorry, Lily." Gently, Silver let go of her hand. "I've failed to protect you – and it's worse because you're the best friend I ever had. She'll drive a stake through my heart – but my heart's broken anyway because I couldn't save you."

Her cold lips kissed Lily's cheek. Then she kissed Oz and Caydon.

"Your trouble," Alba said, "is that you've been ruined by sentimentality." She grabbed Silver with one hand, pinned her against a high joist, and with one single, swift movement, she drove the stake into the vampire's heart.

There was a moment of terrible silence and stillness that

overwhelmed the racket of the bombs and the firestorm outside. Its centre was the pale body of Silver – with the jagged wooden stake sticking out of her rainbow jersey.

Lily began to sob. Oz and Caydon sniffed and dragged their sleeves across their eyes.

Their bodyguard was dead. They held their breath as they waited for her corpse to crumble into dust.

"She's not crumbling," Secunda said. "But the younger ones do tend to last a bit longer."

"We won't wait," Alba said. "This dome will catch fire and collapse at any moment – I'll go back to my boys, ready to grab them the minute the seal is destroyed. B62, make yourself useful."

The oldest of the Emperor Diocletian's awful daughters turned to leave the dome, as if Silver and the other humans were already dust.

Secunda scrambled after her. "And what if the boys carry on refusing to come with you? It's too late to cancel this fire now, and I still want France. I suggest we just leave them to burn with everyone else."

"I'm not burning my children, thank you very much!"

"Hmm," Secunda said. "You weren't so fussy about burning mine."

"What? Oh – you mean those creatures you had after you married the warthog – you would've eaten them yourself eventually. And you must admit, they had a nice crispy glaze."

"I was saving them for my birthday!"

"This is simply unbelievable," Newt's voice piped up, alongside those of the squabbling witches. "Just a few hours ago I was sitting in my office, designing a parade of shops for a site in East Grinstead. And now I'm about to be murdered by witches who eat their own children! I think I must have eaten something queer."

He was chattering happily to himself, sure that he was dreaming. The backs of the two witches were turned and now they hurried away, noticing neither the dazed architect, nor the fact that the snapping fire around the chocolate phoenix had not spread, but glowed above them like a scarlet lantern.

Lily looked at B62, who quickly put a finger to her lips. She felt a flutter of hope and saw it reflected in the eager faces of Oz and Caydon. Could the treacherous B62 be on their side after all?

"The mashed potato was odd tonight," Newt continued. "My landlady's a terrible cook —"

Oz nudged Newt's foot, which was the nearest part of him. "Hey, wake up!"

"— and I suspect her of fiddling my rations."

"Wake up — this isn't a dream!"

"Leave him," B62 said. "He's better off not knowing this is real."

She moved quickly to where Silver's body lay — chalk-white and shrivelled, but still not turned to dust. She pulled something out of the neck of Silver's rainbow jersey and vigorously shook it.

"What are you doing to her?" asked Caydon.

"I know – you're ringing her bell!" Lily said. "But what will that do?"

"It'll bring magical help," said B62. "Though I don't know what kind – it's not making much noise."

Lily said, "It's too late to save Silver, isn't it?"

"I'm sorry," B62 said gently. "I would've stopped her if I could."

"But," Oz said, "I thought you were working for D33 – you were the one who betrayed us."

"I was a plant," B62 said. "They thought I was as wicked as they were because my father was one of their top smugglers. But really I never stopped working for the government."

"I'm glad you're on our side after all." Lily wiped her eyes on her sleeve.

Newt spoke up again. "I'm starting to wonder how much of this is a dream. I can feel the dome shaking—"

"Me too," Oz said. "Is it going to collapse?"

The joists they were sitting on quivered and creaked, and the great dome trembled around them.

"Look!" B62 cried suddenly.

Something dark was boiling and seething and surging along the wooden joists. For one moment Lily thought it was a wave of black water, until she saw that the wave was made of fur. Thousands of cats and rats – all packed together in a wriggling mass – poured through the dome.

A big knot of rats ran to the fire and hurled themselves recklessly on top of it. There was a stench of burning rodent. Several rats began to fight over the chocolate phoenix. Finally they all fell on it at once – and suddenly the phoenix was gone, the rats with it. There was no spark of fire left inside the dome and they were suddenly in deep darkness.

"Half a mo," Newt's voice called cheerfully. "I've got my torch in my pocket. I always carry it because of the blackout."

A thin beam of white light appeared, creating an eerie net of shadows.

"They've eaten the phoenix!" Caydon yelled, above the racket of squeaks and mews and falling bombs. "Did we need it to get home?" He had automatically turned to Silver, and his lip quivered when he saw her corpse.

In the confusion of darkness, Lily saw B62 gently pull the wooden stake out of Silver's chest. She took off her jacket and laid it over the vampire's face.

"I'm so sorry, my dear!" A warm, plump, furry body landed around Lily's shoulders. "Poor Silver was a lovely girl – and such a sensitive beautician! I can give no higher praise."

Lily said, "She was trying to protect us. She could've lived if she'd changed sides. Alba offered her a job."

"But she'd never have done that, dear. She wasn't wicked enough."

"I wouldn't care if she was wicked," Lily said, "if only she could be alive."

"We must get out of here," said B62. "This fire's out, but Alba will soon start another." She hoisted Silver's body on to her shoulder.

Following the bobbing light of Newt's torch, Oz, Lily, Caydon and B62 crawled out of the dome of St Paul's, helped by the army of cats and rats, who half carried, half pushed them back the way they'd come.

The fires around the cathedral were raging harder than ever, and the team of fire watchers on the dome were scrambling into all sorts of dangerous places to get at the incendiary bombs.

Newt shook his head several times, as if he'd just woken up, then stumbled off to help with the bomb-catching. Hundreds of cats and rats swarmed to join him – the rats were particularly good at getting into the hardest places. The fire watchers were too busy to notice anything strange.

Demerara and Spike stayed with the children. They were standing on a wide gutter that ran right around the bottom of the great dome.

"I'm going to try to get you lot home," B62 called to them above the noise. "I'll stay to make sure the fire doesn't reach the cathedral, but you lot have done enough and it's not safe for you without a bodyguard." She laid Silver's body down on the lead floor of the gutter. "The reverend should be able to help us."

Lily was exhausted with crying for her friend, but there was a little bit of comfort in hearing the word "home".

"If we've still got homes in the future," Caydon said tensely. "If it hasn't been turned into Alba's horrible new world."

The words were barely out of his mouth when a tremor ran under their feet, and then another. The dome was moving.

"Get against the wall!" shouted B62. "Hold on as tight as you can!"

"She's done it!" Oz gasped. "It's collapsing!"

The thought hung between the three of them. This was the end; they were going to die in the ruins of St Paul's in 1940, and they would never see their homes again.

The dome was shifting alarmingly now. Lily, Oz and Caydon clung to the wall and to each other, while B62 tried to shield them with her body.

And then something happened that was beyond anything else imaginable.

The immense dome of St Paul's bucked violently under their feet and they all screamed as the whole thing lifted up and tilted them backwards. The dome had risen like a great lid – and something was poking out underneath it.

Through the smoke and the storm of sparks, they saw an enormous dirty hand. Its vast fingers were clasped around something black.

"BOYS!" screamed the voice of Alba. "Stop being naughty and put us down AT ONCE!"

"I TOLD you they didn't like you!" raged the voice of Secunda. "I'm GLAD you lost that bloody phoenix – time travelling with you is RUBBISH!"

The vast hand opened. A gigantic and filthy fingernail flicked the two witches far off into the night sky. A second later, one of the enemy planes exploded above their heads.

There was a sickening lurch as the dome crashed back into place.

"Well, I'll be blowed," squeaked Spike. "Those idiotic giants were on our side after all!"

24

Death of a Vampire

It didn't feel like a victory. The planes had gone and the bombing had stopped, but the firestorm was still tearing through the City of London.

And Silver was still dead.

Lily felt as if someone had scraped out her insides and left her hollow. She couldn't look at her friend's body. She tried touching one of her arms; it was as hard and cold as stone under the uneven rainbow sleeve.

"Come on." B62 put a hand on her shoulder.

"We can't leave Silver. I won't leave her."

"Of course not. I'll carry her." Once again B62 hauled Silver over one shoulder. "Now go with the boys."

Lily followed Oz and Caydon back through the door, down the endless stairs, into the magnificent interior of the cathedral – which looked none the worse for having its roof lifted off by a pair of giants.

The ghostly Mr Prout was waiting for them. "Well done, that was marvellous work."

"We didn't do anything in the end," Caydon said. "We weren't needed – the giants did it."

"You're quite wrong, my boy. The very fact that you three were here undermined Alba's power, and there seems to be some strange affinity between the giants and yourselves. You're distantly related, of course. They're carriers of the D33 gene, like you."

Caydon was startled. "Related – to those morons?"

"That's a little severe," Mr Prout said, smiling. "As they've shown, they have a strong sense of loyalty – except to their mother, I'm glad to say."

"Excuse me," asked B62. "Is there a working portal in this cathedral?"

"Certainly" – the old ghost became businesslike – "if you're able to operate magic at that level." He glanced at Silver and sighed. "I'm very sorry about this vampire child. I shall be thinking of her poor parents."

For the first time since coming here, Lily had begun to believe that they really might be going home. Her heart beat uncomfortably to think of the joy of being back with Mum and Dad and Daisy – but it hurt to remember Cathy and Vaz.

In a sorrowful, battered, sooty group, they followed the

gliding figure of Mr Prout along the aisle of the cathedral, to a plain wooden door in the wall. This time they were not returning to their own century down a toilet; this door opened straight out into the fiery night air, yet as each of them passed through it, the time stream caught them and whipped them into the hurricane of history.

And then there was a stunning silence, shocking as a blow.

The hurricane died down and they were sprawled across a concrete floor, in a huge space that was lit by sickly electric light.

"I think" – B62 sat up, shaking her head – "I'm pretty sure this is the SMU car park, underneath the MI6 building."

Oz dragged himself upright. "When?"

"I don't care," Caydon said. "As long as the war's over."

"We're back in the right time," B62 said. "I can see my Renault Clio."

"Does that mean it's all OK?"

"Silver!" Lily choked suddenly. With a shaking finger, she pointed at Silver's body, lying under B62's jacket. "She – moved!"

"My poor dear," purred Demerara, rubbing against her legs. "I know it's hard to believe. When our human owner died, Spike and I were constantly imagining we heard him."

"I didn't imagine it!"

Everyone stared at Silver.

From under the jacket came a long, deep sigh.

"She's still alive!" Oz gasped.

B62 crawled over to Silver and quickly uncovered her face. The vampire's eyes were closed – but her face was no longer pinched and shrivelled. It was strangely pink and plump, and she looked as if she were sleeping peacefully.

"Oh my G—" B62's face was now whiter than Silver's. She scrambled in her pocket for her phone and gabbled into it. "This is an emergency Code Nine for Area Six – I need an ambulance with a vampire crash team NOW!"

Silver opened her eyes and yawned. "Have I been asleep?"

"Silver!" Lily cried. "You're not dead!"

"Dead? Of course I'm not dead – actually, I feel fantastic."

She tried to sit up but B62 pushed her back to the floor. "Lie down and don't move; you've been very seriously injured."

Spike scuttled over to pat Silver's hair with his paw. "You've had a stake driven through your heart and I know how that feels! You want to take it easy for a minute."

"Good gracious, what a fright you gave us!" Demerara rubbed her furry cheek against Silver's hand. "I'm afraid your clothes are in absolute shreds, my dear."

"Maybe the stake missed your heart," B62 said, wide-eyed with amazement. "But I don't see how — I saw the terrible wound in your chest!"

"My chest's fine." Silver glanced down at the blackened mess of her front, and smiled. "There's a terrible wound in my jersey — but I can live with that."

Oz said, "It's good to have you back, Silver."

"It's great," Caydon said. "I've got used to having you around, Major Biggins."

"Are you really alive?" asked Lily. She had never felt such relief, such happiness; the thought of life without her best friend had been horrible.

"I keep telling you, I'm fine! In fact, I haven't felt this fine in years! I don't know where we are but the air down here is lovely. It's filling me with energy — and I could murder a burger!"

"Me too," Caydon said. "But, hang on, you don't eat meat."

"Don't I? I really fancy some now. Or some of that cottage pie your gran was cooking the other day."

"There's something different about you." Lily looked at Silver more closely. "You're sort of younger. Your teeth are smaller. And you're bleeding — there's a cut on your hand."

"Bleeding?" For the first time, Silver was rattled. She looked at the red cut on her hand. "But that's not possible!"

"Lie still," said B62. "The crash team's here."

On the other side of the underground car park there was a commotion of doors banging and feet running. Four paramedics dashed across the concrete floor, wheeling a stretcher and hefting boxes of medical equipment.

Silver's parents were with them, their faces white and anguished.

"Hi, Mum," Silver said. "Hi, Dad."

"Silver!" Cathy gasped. "What's going on? They told us—"

"Mrs Biggins, I must ask you to stand well back." A very smartly dressed man, in a black suit and black bow tie, firmly pushed Silver's mother aside. He knelt down beside Silver. "Hello, do you remember me? I'm Dr LeStrange from the vampire clinic."

"Yes, of course I remember you," Silver said. "You gave me an injection last month. What's going on? This is getting embarrassing! And why are you dressed like Count Dracula?"

"It's the evening," Dr LeStrange said. "I was at a gala fundraising dinner. Take a deep breath, please."

He listened to Silver's heart through his stethoscope. He peered down her throat and shone lights in her eyes. He got out a magnifying glass and stared for a long time at the cut on her hand.

"Well?" Cathy asked. "What's happened to her? Why won't you tell me anything?"

"I've never seen anything like this before." The doctor was deadly serious and his eyes glittered with excitement. "It's quite incredible! Amazing! Stand up, please."

"OK." Silver scrambled quickly to her feet.

"I want to test your vampire strength. Go and pick up that car over there."

Silver went over to the nearest car – B62's Renault Clio – and tried to pick it up. She couldn't shift it. "This is weird – I feel stronger than I have in ages, but I haven't any actual strength!"

Dr LeStrange grinned. "Now walk up this wall, and walk down head first."

They were all silent now. Silver ran to the wall, and immediately landed in a heap at the bottom. "Ow – I can't do it!"

"She's lost her powers!" Cathy whispered. "What does it mean? Is it serious?"

"It's extremely serious," Dr LeStrange said. "I'll need to do some follow-up tests, but there's no mistaking it. Mr and Mrs Biggins, please prepare yourselves for a shock."

Vaz whispered, "How long has she got?"

"I'd say about eighty years." The vampire doctor was smiling. "In other words, a normal, healthy human life span. Young lady, you've just made history – you're not a vampire any more."

25

Blessings and Curses

There was a stunned silence – and no one was more stunned than Silver and her parents.

"If I'm not a vampire," Silver said, "what am I?"

"A healthy human girl of eleven years." The doctor made a sign to the paramedics, who began to take the emergency paraphernalia away. "It's quite extraordinary, and it's never happened before. This might even mean a breakthrough in the treatment."

"You mean," Silver whispered, "I'm – normal?"

Cathy buried her head in her arms and burst into loud sobs.

"Oh, man!" murmured Vaz. "Oh, wow!"

"But what'll happen to me now? Am I fired from the SMU?"

B62 suddenly looked years younger; her eyes were shining. "You can't be in the Vampire Unit when you're not a vampire. You'll be too busy being a normal eleven-year-old."

"Proper food and proper school!" Silver said, dazed. "And I'll have to move up a year, for the first time in more than two centuries!"

Lily, Oz and Caydon looked at one another uncertainly, not sure how to react.

Caydon said, "So you won't be able to pick me up and hold me over your head?"

"No. My superhuman strength has gone. Now I'm only about as strong as you are."

"Well, that works for me!" He grinned at her. "Welcome back to the human race."

"Thanks," Silver said. She put her arm around Cathy. "Mum, are you all right?"

"All right?" Cathy leapt joyfully to her feet. "This is the happiest day of my life since you were born!" She hugged Silver. "Vaz, look at our darling girl — as fresh and young as the day Fanny bit her!"

Vaz beamed behind his beard. "You'll grow up! You'll get tall and move up the school — Mum and I can go to parents' evenings! But the first thing I'm going to do is knit you a new jersey."

"Thanks, Dad." Silver grinned and rolled her eyes at Lily. "I might even wear it."

"And I'm going to send a text to poor old Fanny," said Cathy. "She'll be over the moon. She always felt so terrible about biting you."

"My dear Silver," Demerara purred, rubbing herself against the ex-vampire's legs. "How wonderful that you're not dead after all! Just wait till you hear what happened while you were dead in 1940. . . Without a thought for my own safety (and with a tiny bit of help from Spike) I led the cats of London to a glorious victory and I'm pretty likely to get a HUGE medal. Now, what does a cat have to do to get something to EAT in this place?"

"And what happened to the chocolate phoenix?" Silver asked. "Did we leave it inside the dome of St Paul's?"

"Oh, of course, you missed that bit when you were dead," Lily said. "A load of rats ate it, and just disappeared."

Silver giggled. "I wonder where they went?"

"They could've shown up anywhere," Spike squeaked, from Oz's shoulder. "But they won't have noticed any difference. Any time is much the same to your average rat." He burped. "Beg pardon, I must've had too many chips."

B62 had taken Silver's parents off for a meeting with J, and Rosie from the commando unit had appeared in the underground car park to take the children and animals to the SMU canteen. They had all been hungry, but Silver had been ravenous. She'd wolfed down a large burger and so many chips that even Caydon was impressed.

"I can't describe how great this tastes," she had told Lily. "This is the first food I've tasted in more than two hundred years. Being alive again feels like waking up after the world's longest night."

After the food, they had been taken to the secret kennels in Muswell Hill – and it had been delightful to look out of the windows at the streets of London, clean and cheerful and not being consumed by flames. The SMU had done a magnificent job restoring the high street, and it was hard to believe it had ever been devastated by a rampaging stegosaurus.

They were now in a waiting area in an underground corridor, feeling light-hearted and a bit silly after the excitement – especially Silver, who was becoming more like an ordinary eleven-year-old girl every moment.

"You know what, Lily, your short hair looks rather good. I'd copy it myself but my hair's paler than yours and I'm afraid I'd just look bald – which is only a good look on Daisy."

They all laughed at this, mainly because it was nice to think about Daisy.

Oz said, "I hope we can go home soon."

"Not long now." B62 came along the corridor, wheeling a trolley. She had changed out of her torn, burnt clothes and looked very cheerful. "J's caught up in a complicated meeting, but he'll be free in a few minutes."

"Are those Mars Bars?" Silver asked. "Could I have one?"

"Of course – this trolley is for the class, but there are plenty."

There were several classes going on behind the closed white doors along the corridor. Silver took a Mars Bar, and just then one of the doors opened.

Three old ladies came out, followed by a man of about Lily's dad's age, and then a tall, skinny woman with a sorry tangle of half-burnt grey hair.

"Greta!" Lily cried. "How are you?"

"Oh, hello, Lily." Greta might have been bedraggled, but her face was beaming and she looked years younger. "What are you doing here? I'm here because Mummy's having her Evil Management class."

Dr Spatz – now clean and tidy, with his white beard shaved off – appeared behind her. "Our class is called Evil Anonymous – it's a group for relatives of the magically evil."

Greta lowered her voice and nodded towards a nearby door. "The evil ones are in there. They have to keep Evil Diaries and write down their feelings whenever they have an attack."

"Twelvey hasn't quite got the hang of it yet," Dr Spatz said, helping himself to a cup of tea. "She keeps losing her temper and incinerating her diary. But Rome wasn't built in a day."

"Are we still going to have lessons with you?" Lily asked.

"Certainly," Greta said. "We have a lot of catching up to do. We'll start again next Saturday – and Mummy's promised to do some new flavours of magic milkshake."

"Well, Silver," Demerara purred, "that makes Saturday afternoon the ideal time for my next beauty treatment. I couldn't help noticing your mother's nail polish; perhaps you can borrow it for me."

Silver laughed. "Yes, your majesty!"

"There's no need to be sarcastic, my dear. Sarcasm isn't nice in an eleven-year-old."

"You know I love giving you treatments." Silver bent down to pat the cat's soft golden bottom. "And you've been so brave that you deserve something special."

"Hmm," Demerara said thoughtfully. "I wonder if now is the time for a perm? Or should I tint my fur a shade more blonde? I've always thought highlights would suit me."

B62 glanced at a text on her phone. "We can go in now."

Lily hugged Greta, and they followed B62 to an underground office, where they found J with a thin woman in thick spectacles who barely looked round when they came in.

"I find it very hard to approve of this," she was saying. "It could upset years of vital research."

"I'm sorry, Dr Flanagan," J said. "I've made up my mind. But all your conditions will be met." He smiled when he saw the children and animals. "Ah, my favourite agents!" They had never seen him so jolly. "You remember Dr Flanagan?"

"I certainly do," Demerara hissed. "She's the ghastly woman who tried to leave me in that dinosaur's stomach!"

Dr Flanagan stood up stiffly. "It's a shame the department has been swayed by pure sentimentality. I'd better start the arrangements at once."

"Thank you, Dr Flanagan."

Dr Flanagan left the room, shooting a cross look at Demerara.

"What's up with her?" Oz asked, once the door had slammed shut.

"Nothing to worry about," J said. "She's unhappy because I've decided to move Steggy. He'll be joining his old owners underneath St Paul's. I thought those giants deserved a reward."

"Hope they don't eat him," Caydon said.

"Dr Flanagan's fretting about her research programme," J went on. "But when she calms down, she'll see what a good deal she's got out of me – two more full-time palaeontologists on her staff, and a special dinosaur dungeon with exercise facilities. If he wasn't so happy about London being saved, the prime minister would be horrified by the expense."

"I think Steggy will love it," Oz said. "He must've been bored in that cage."

"I think Gog and Magog will love it too," Caydon said. "Whichever one of them I was in my vision, he really loved his pet."

"The SMU authorities at St Paul's are delighted to have Steggy," J said. "Mr Prout's still there, by the way, and says hello."

"Still there? Oh, of course – he's a ghost," Silver said. "Weird to think that we could visit him right now if we liked."

"He says pop round any time," J said. "You've all done a fantastic job. I can't thank you enough."

Oz suddenly remembered something. "You said you might not be here when we came back. But you are here."

J chuckled. "I shouldn't tell you, but I think you can be trusted not to blow my cover. You see, if St Paul's had burned down that night, everyone working there would have been killed. And one of them was my father – I would never have been born."

"Where was your father?" Lily asked. "What did he look like?"

"You met him, I think," J said. "He was an architect."

"We met a young guy called Newt," Caydon said.

"Yes, that was him – he married the nurse whose

uniform was stolen by Alba. And his witch-spotting talent got him a job in the SMU Intelligence section at Bletchley Park. B62, could you open the champagne?"

B62 smiled, and moved to a fridge in the corner to take out a bottle of champagne, and fizzy apple juice for the children. "Don't worry – it won't be drugged this time!"

"I'm glad you're not really working for D33," Lily said. "It was horrible when we thought you were a traitor."

"I hated having to pretend to be working with them. Shall I give the animals some champagne, sir?"

"I wouldn't say no," Spike said.

"Just a teeny drop," Demerara said, "for my poor nerves as much as anything."

B62 opened the champagne and splashed some into two saucers for Demerara and Spike, who began lapping it up at once.

"You two did very well," J said. "Thanks to you, the cats and rats of London managed to save the city – without fighting."

"Thank you, sir!" Spike burped. "Pardon!"

"Spike, must you be so crude?"

"Come on, old girl – I said pardon, didn't I?"

"And Silver." J leaned across his desk to look kindly at the vampire girl. "Before all this, I'd have included you in the champagne. But it's rather different now."

"What will happen to me?" asked Silver.

They'd all been too excited about being safe in the present to think about this. The job was over, and normally that would mean that Silver and her parents were sent off somewhere else.

J said, "You can't be a major in the vampire unit, I'm afraid."

"No, I suppose not." Silver hung her head. "Am I – fired?"

"Not quite. Now that you're no longer a vampire, you've been demoted. You're now a human girl with a gift for seeing certain strange things."

"That's all? You mean, I'll be like Lily?"

"More or less," J said. "In fact, Lily, Oz and Caydon now have more magic than you do. And you may gradually forget the details of all your years as a vampire."

Silver's smile grew slowly, until her face was radiant. "Do you mean I'll have an ordinary life, just going to school and doing stuff with my friends? That's the most wonderful thing I've ever heard!"

"You'll be staying at Sir Richard Whittington School," J said. "We've decided to turn the house at Plum Terrace into a permanent safe house, and I've put Cathy and Vaz in charge."

This was brilliant news. Lily and Silver gasped aloud with joy. At last they could just be normal, a-little-bit-magic best friends, living round the corner from each other and having sleepovers at each other's houses.

"You'll be able to play with Daisy as much as you like now," Lily said.

"And ordinary cats will let you stroke them again," Demerara added. "Your vampire smell has quite gone."

"The vampire clinic will want to examine you thoroughly, for research purposes," J said. "Dr LeStrange thinks the wood at St Paul's might have special healing properties, which would explain why it couldn't kill you."

"Maybe they'll discover a cure," Lily said. "All because of you."

"Is that possible, sir?" asked Silver.

"It's too early to say – but, yes, it's very promising. Apart from the medical tests, however, the SMU won't be bothering you until you're grown up. Your last order is to go off and be an eleven-year-old."

Skittle Street looked beautiful when they got back. The ghostly soldiers had gone, and the pale autumn sun made the heaps of fruit outside the supermarket gleam like jewels.

"It's good to be home," Silver said. "It's so fantastic to have a real home at last. Plum Terrace is the nicest place we've ever been."

Elvira was outside, taking a bag of rubbish to the bins. "Welcome back!"

Caydon ran to give her an enormous hug. "Great to see you, Gran! We did it – though I don't know exactly what we did—"

"It's just like I said." Elvira was smiling. "There's a lot of magic around here, especially since Daisy arrived. I somehow knew nothing really bad could happen while she was here — even Madge Fladgate could see how special she is."

"Let's go and see her," Lily said. "It's nearly her bath-time."

Lily and Silver went into Number 18.

"Well?" Oz asked Caydon. "How about some motor racing in my bedroom?"

"Not half!" Spike's head popped out of Caydon's pocket. "I've lost a bit of weight, what with saving London — I bet I can beat that red car now!"

"Yeah, OK." A shadow had fallen across Caydon's face at the mention of Mrs Fladgate.

"What's the matter?"

"He's just thinking about that terrible prediction she made!" Elvira — rather to Oz's surprise — gave a great chortle of laughter as she went back into her flat.

"You don't have to tell me," Oz said. "But it can't be all that serious, if your gran thinks it's funny."

Caydon scowled. "It's not funny — got that?"

"There's no need to take it out on me!"

"Sorry. It's not your fault." He let out a deep sigh. "If I tell you what that old bag said, you have to SWEAR you'll never tell anyone."

"I swear."

Caydon leaned close to Oz and whispered in his ear, "She said that when I grow up, I'm – I'm – going to marry Lily."

Oz was shocked – it was weird to think of his twin sister marrying anyone. But if she had to get married, he couldn't help thinking it would be good to have Caydon as a brother-in-law. And it was a relief to know that the prediction wasn't life-threatening.

"Well," he said slowly. "That's not SO bad—"

"Huh!"

"And it won't happen for ages, if it does happen."

Caydon looked at him crossly, and then his face cleared and he smiled. "You're right – it's stupid to worry about it now. Let's go and give Spike that workout!"

Don't miss Oz and Lily's first adventure...

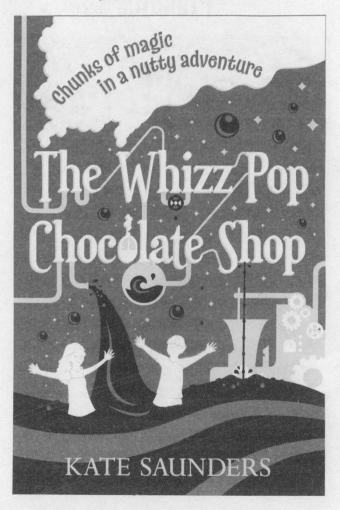

chunks of magic in a nutty adventure

The Whizz Pop Chocolate Shop

KATE SAUNDERS

If you liked The Curse of the Chocolate Phoenix you'll love. . .

Beswitched

"The new
Eva Ibbotson"
Amanda Craig

KATE SAUNDERS

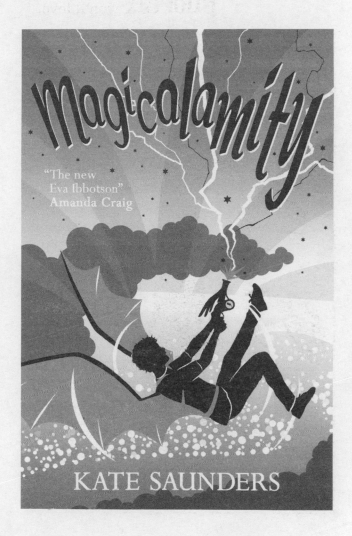

"The new
Eva Ibbotson"
Amanda Craig

KATE SAUNDERS